The Author

Enid Blyton

Enid Blyton is one of the best-loved writers of the twentieth century. Her wonderful, inventive stories, plays and poems have delighted children of all ages for generations.

Born in London in 1897, Enid Blyton sold her first piece of literature; a poem entitled 'Have You …?' at the age of twenty. She qualified and worked as a teacher, writing extensively in her spare time. She sold short stories and poems to various magazines and her first book, *Child Whispers*, was published in 1922.

Over the next 40 years, Blyton would publish on average fifteen books a year. Some of her more famous works include *Noddy*, *The Famous Five*, *The Secret Seven* and *The Faraway Tree* series.

Her books have sold in the millions and have been translated into many languages. Enid Blyton married twice and had two daughters. She died in 1968, but her work continues to live on.

Contents

The Bed That Took a Walk

The pixie Miggle was always late for everything. If he went to catch a train he had to run all the way and then he would miss it. If he went to catch a bus it had always gone round the corner before he got there.

'It's just as easy to be early as to be late,' said his friends. 'Why don't you get up a bit sooner, then you would be in time for everything?'

'Well, I'm so sleepy in the mornings,' said Miggle. My wife comes and calls me, but I go off to sleep again. I really am a very tired person in the morning.'

'Lazy, he means!' said his friends to one another. 'Never in time for anything! It's shocking. One day he will be very sorry.'

In the month of June the King and Queen of the pixies were coming to visit Apple Tree Town, where Miggle and his friends lived. The pixies were very excited.

'I shall get a new coat,' said Jinky.

'I shall buy a new feather for my hat,' said Twinkle.

'I shall have new red shoes,' said Flitter.

'And I shall buy a whole new suit, a new hat and feathers, and new shoes and buckles with the money I have saved up,' said Miggle. 'I shall be very grand indeed!'

'You'll never be in time to see the King and Queen!' said Jinky, with a laugh.

'Indeed I shall,' said Miggle. 'I shall be up before any of you that day.'

Well, the day before the King and Queen came, Miggle was very busy trying on his new things. The coat didn't quite fit so he asked his wife to alter it. She stayed up very late trying to make it right.

It was about midnight when Miggle got to bed. How he yawned! 'Wake me up at seven o'clock' he said. 'Don't forget.'

Mrs Miggle was tired. 'I shall call you three times, and then, if you don't get up, I shan't call you any more,' she said. '*I* have to call myself—nobody calls *me*—and I am tired tonight, so I shall not be very patient with you tomorrow if you don't get up when I call you.'

'You *do* sound cross,' said Miggle, and got into bed. He fell fast asleep, and it seemed no time at all before he felt Mrs Miggle shouting in his ear, and shaking him.

'Miggle! It's seven o'clock. Miggle get up!'

'All right,' said Miggle, and turned over to go to sleep again. In five minutes time Mrs Miggle shook him again, and once more he woke up, and went to sleep again.

'This is the third time I've called you,' said Mrs Miggle, 10 minutes later, in a cross voice. 'And it's the last time. If you don't get up now, I shan't call you any more.'

'Right,' said Miggle. 'Just getting up, my dear.' But he didn't. He went to sleep again. Plenty of time to get up and dress and go and see the King and Queen!

Mrs Miggle kept her word. She didn't call Miggle again. She got dressed in her best frock and went to meet the King and Queen. Miggle slept on soundly, not hearing the footsteps going down the road, as all the pixies hurried by to meet the royal pair.

Miggle's bed creaked to wake him. It shook a little, but Miggle didn't stir. The bed was cross. It thought Miggle stayed too long in it. It knew how upset Miggle would be when he woke up and found that the King and Queen had gone.

So it thought it would take Miggle to the Town Hall, where the King and Queen would be, and perhaps he would wake up there.

The bed walked on its four legs to the door. It squeezed itself through, for it was a narrow bed. It trotted down the street, clickity-clack, clickity-clack.

Miggle didn't wake. He had a lovely dream that he was in a boat that went gently up and down on the sea, and said 'clickity-clack' all the time.

'Gracious! Look, isn't that Miggle asleep on that bed?' cried Jinky, with a squeal of laughter. 'The bed is wide awake, but Miggle isn't—so the bed is taking him to the Town Hall!'

'Clickity-clack, clickity-clack,' went the four legs of the bed. Miggle gave a little snore. He was warm and cosy and comfy, and as fast asleep as ever.

The bed made its way into the Town Hall just as the King and Queen came on to the stage to speak to their people. The pixies jumped to their feet and cheered loudly.

The bed jumped up and down in joy, because it was enjoying the treat too. Miggle woke up when he heard the cheering, and felt the bumping of the bed. He sat up and looked round in the greatest surprise.

3

'Ha ha, ho ho, look at Miggle,' shouted everyone, and the King and Queen had to smile too. Miggle was full of horror and shame! What had happened! Had his silly bed brought him to the Town Hall? Oh dear, and he was in his pyjamas too, instead of in his lovely new clothes!

Miggle could have wept with shame. Mrs Miggle saw him and went over to him. 'Really Miggle! To think you've come to see the King and Queen in bed, not even dressed! I'm ashamed of you! What *can* you be thinking of?'

Miggle slid down into bed and pulled the clothes over his head. Mrs Miggle pulled them off.

'Now you get up and bow properly to His Majesty the King and Her Majesty the Queen,' she said.

'What, in my pyjamas?' said poor Miggle.

'Well, if you've come in pyjamas, you'll have to bow in them,' said Mrs Miggle. So Miggle had to stand up on the bed in his pyjamas and bow to the King and Queen. How they laughed!

'What a funny man!' said the Queen. 'Does he often do things like this?'

Miggle didn't know what to do. He lay down again and ordered the bed to go home. But the bed wasn't a dog, to be ordered here and there. It wanted to stay and see the fun.

So Miggle had to jump out and run all the way home in his pyjamas. 'How dreadful, how dreadful!' he kept thinking, as he ran. 'I can't bear it! I'd better put on all my fine clothes, and go back and let the King and Queen see how grand I really am!'

So he did—but alas, when he got back to the Town Hall, the King and Queen had just gone. Everyone was coming away, pleased and excited. Miggle's bed trotted with them, 'clickity-clack'.

'Hallo, Miggle? Going to ride home asleep in bed?' cried his friends. 'Oh, how you made the King and Queen laugh! It was the funniest sight we've ever seen.'

Miggle frowned and didn't say a word. His bed tried to walk close to him, but he wouldn't let it. Horrid bed! 'I'll never be late again!' thought Miggle. 'Never, never, never!'

But he will. It's not so easy to get out of a bad habit. Won't it be funny if his bed walks off with him again?

Brownie's Magic

One night the snow came. It fell quietly all night through, and in the morning, what a surprise for everyone! The hills were covered with snow. The trees were white. The bushes were hidden, and the whole world looked strange and magical.

Bobbo the brownie looked out of his cave in the hill-side. The path down to the little village was hidden now. The path that ran over the top of the hill had gone too.

'Snow everywhere,' said Bobbo. 'Beautiful white snow! How I love it! I wish I had watched it falling last night, like big white goose feathers.'

He saw someone coming up the hill, and he waved to him.

'Ah!' he said, 'there is my clever cousin, Brownie Bright-Eyes. I wonder what he has brought to show me today. He is always bringing me wonderful things.'

Brownie Bright-Eyes walked up the hill in the snow, making deep footprints as he came, for he carried something large and heavy.

'What have you got there?' said Bobbo, when Bright-Eyes at last came to his cave. 'You are always bringing me something strange and wonderful to see, Bright-Eyes.'

'I have made a marvellous mirror,' panted Bright-Eyes, bringing the shining glass into the cave. 'I do think I am clever, Bobbo. I made this magic mirror myself. I think I must be the cleverest brownie in the world.'

'Don't boast,' said Bobbo. 'I don't like you when you boast.'

'I am not boasting!' cried Bright-Eyes crossly. 'Wait till you do something clever yourself, and then scold me for boasting. It's a pity you don't use your own brains.'

'I do,' said Bobbo. 'But you are always so full of your own wonderful doings that you never listen to me when I want to tell you something.'

'I don't expect you would have anything half so wonderful to tell me as I have to tell you,' said Bright-Eyes. 'Now—just look at this mirror.'

Bobbo looked at it. It was a strange mirror, because it didn't reflect what was in front of it. It was just dark, with a kind of mist moving in the glass. Bobbo could see that it was very magic.

'I can't see anything,' said Bobbo.

'No, you can't—but if you want to know where anyone is—Tippy the brownie for instance—the mirror will show you!'

'What do you mean?' asked Bobbo, astonished.

'Now look,' said Bright-Eyes. He stroked the shining mirror softly. 'Mirror, mirror, show me where Tippy the brownie is!'

And at once a strange thing happened. The mist in the glass slowly cleared away—and there was Tippy the brownie, sitting in a bus. The mirror showed him quite clearly.

'Isn't that wonderful?' said Bright-Eyes. 'You couldn't possibly have told me where Tippy was, without the help of the mirror, could you?'

'Yes, I could,' said Bobbo. 'I knew he was in the bus.'

'You didn't!' said Bright-Eyes.

'I did,' said Bobbo.

'Then you must have seen Tippy this morning,' said Bright-Eyes.

'I haven't,' said Bobbo. '*You* found out where he was by using your magic mirror, but I, Bright-Eyes, I found out by using my brains! So I am cleverer than you.'

Bright-Eyes didn't like that. He always wanted to be the cleverest person anywhere. He frowned at Bobbo.

'I expect it was just a guess on your part that Tippy was in the bus,' he said. 'Now—can you tell me where Jinky is—you know, the pixie who lives down the hill?'

'Yes,' said Bobbo at once. 'He's gone up the hill to see his aunt, who lives over the top.'

Bright-Eyes rubbed the mirror softly. 'Mirror, mirror show me where Jinky is!' he said. And at once the mirror showed him a pixie, sitting in a chair, talking to a plump old lady. It was Jinky, talking to his aunt!

'There you are, you see—I was right,' said Bobbo, pleased. 'I am cleverer than your mirror. It uses magic— but I use my brains. I can tell you a lot of things that *you* could only get to know through your magic mirror—but which *I* know by using my very good brains. Ha, ha!'

'What can you tell me?' asked Bright-Eyes.

'I can tell you that Red-Coat the fox passed by here in the night, although I did not see or hear him,' said Bobbo. 'I can tell you that six rabbits played in the snow down the hill this morning. I can tell you that Mother

Jane's ducks left the frozen pond today and went to her garden to be fed.'

'You must have seen them all. That's easy,' said Bright-Eyes.

'I tell you, I have not seen anything or anyone today except you,' said Bobbo. 'I know all this by using my brains.'

'What else do you know?' asked Bright-Eyes, thinking that Bobbo must really be cleverer than he thought.

'I know that the sparrows flew down to peck crumbs that Mother Jane scattered for them,' said Bobbo. 'I know that Crek-Crek the moorhen took a walk by the side of the pond. I know that Mother Jane's cat ran away from Tippy's dog this morning. And I know that Tippy's cow wandered from its shed, and then went back to it.'

Bright-Eyes stared at Bobbo in wonder. 'You are very clever to know all this, if you did not see anyone,' he said. 'I shall ask my magic mirror if what you say is true!'

He stroked the glass and asked it many things—and each time the glass showed him that what Bobbo said was true! There was the cat chasing the dog. There was the moorhen walking over the snow. There was Tippy's cow wandering all about!

'Please tell me your magic,' said Bright-Eyes to Bobbo. 'It must be very good magic to tell you all these things.'

'Well—come outside and I will show you how I know them all,' said Bobbo, beginning to laugh. They went outside, and Bobbo pointed to the crisp white snow. There were many marks and prints in it as clear as could be.

'Look,' said Bobbo, pointing to some small footprints that showed little pointed toes. 'Tippy always wears pointed shoes—and do you see how deep his footprints are? That shows that he was running. Why was he running? To catch the bus! That's how I knew where he was, without having seen him.'

'How did you know about Jinky going to see his aunt?'' asked Bright-Eyes.

Bobbo pointed to some very big footprints. 'Those are Jinky's marks,' he said 'He has enormous feet. The footprints are going up the hill, and the only person Jinky goes to see over the top is his aunt. So I knew where Jinky was!'

'Very clever,' said Bright-Eyes.

'And I knew that Red-Coat the fox had passed in the night because there are *his* footprints,' said Bobbo, pointing to a set of rather dog-like marks that showed the print of claws very clearly. 'I knew it was Red-Coat because I saw the mark his tail made here and there behind his hind feet—see it?'

'Bright-Eyes saw the mark of the fox's tail in the snow, and the line of footprints too. Bobbo took Bright-Eyes farther down the hill. He showed him the rabbit-prints—little marks for the front feet and longer, bigger ones for the strong hind feet. He showed him where Mother Jane's ducks had walked from the pond to her garden.

'You can see they were ducks because they have left behind them the mark of their webbed feet,' he said. 'And you can see where the sparrows fed because they have left little prints in pairs—they hop, you see, they don't walk or run—so their prints are always in pairs.'

'And there are the moorhen's marks,' said Bright-Eyes. 'He has big feet rather like the old hen at home, although he is a waterbird. But he runs on land as well as swims on water, so he doesn't have webbed feet. Look how he puts them one in front of the other, Bobbo, so the footprints are in a straight line!'

'And there are the marks made by Tippy's cow,' said Bobbo. 'You can tell each hoofmark quite well. And Mother Jane's cat ran *here*—look at the neat little marks. And Tippy's dog ran *here*—you can tell the difference, because the cat puts her claws in when she runs, so they don't show in her footprints, but the dog doesn't—so his *do* show!'

'Bobbo, you are very, very clever,' said Bright-Eyes. 'You are cleverer than I am. It is better to use your eyes and your brains, than to use a magic mirror! I think you are the cleverest brownie in the world!'

Would you like to be as clever as Bobbo? Well, go out into the snow, when it comes, and read the footprints you find there! You will soon know quite a lot.

Dame Lucky's Umbrella

Dame Lucky had a nice yellow umbrella that she liked very much. It had a strange handle. It was in the shape of a bird's head, and very nice to hold.

Dame Lucky had been given it for her last birthday. Her brother had given it to her. 'Now don't go lending this to anyone,' he said. 'You're such a kindly, generous soul that you will lend anything to anyone. But this is such a nice umbrella that I shall be very sad if you lose it.'

'I won't lose it' said Dame Lucky. 'I shall be very, very careful with it. It's the nicest one I've ever had.'

She used it two or three times in the rain and was very pleased with it because it opened out big and wide and kept every spot of rain from her clothes.

Then the summer came and there was no rain to bother about for weeks. Dame Lucky put her umbrella safely away in her wardrobe.

One morning in September her friend, Mother Lucy, came to see her. 'Well, well, this *is* a surprise,' said Dame Lucky. 'You've been so ill that I never thought you'd be allowed to come all this way to see me!'

'Oh, I'm much better,' said Mother Lucy. 'I mustn't stay long, though, because I have to get on to my sister's for lunch. She's expecting me in half an hour.'

But when Mother Lucy got up to go she looked at the sky in dismay. 'Oh, goodness—it's just going to pour with rain. Here are the first drops. I haven't brought an umbrella with me and I shall get soaked.'

'Dear me, you mustn't get wet after being so ill,' said Dame Lucky at once. 'You wait a moment. I'll get my new umbrella. But don't lose it, Lucy, because it's the only one I have and it's very precious.'

'Thank you. You're a kind soul,' said Mother Lucy. Dame Lucky fetched the yellow umbrella and put it up for her. Then off went Mother Lucy to her sister's, quite dry in the pouring rain.

She had a nice lunch at her sister's—and, will you believe it, when she left she quite forgot to take Dame

'You're a kind soul,' said Mother Lucy.

13

Lucky's umbrella with her, because it had stopped raining and the sun was shining.

So there it stood in the umbrella-stand, whilst Mother Hannah waved goodbye to her sister Lucy.

In a little while it began to pour with rain again. Old Mr Kindly had come to call on Mother Hannah without an umbrella and he asked her to lend him one when he was ready to go home.

'You may take any of the umbrellas in the stand,' said Mother Hannah. 'There are plenty there.'

So what did Mr Kindly do but choose the yellow umbrella with the bird-handle, the one that belonged to Dame Lucky! Off he went with it, thinking what a fine one it was and how well it kept the rain off.

When he got home his little grand-daughter was there, waiting for him. 'Oh, Granddad! Can you lend me an umbrella?' she cried. 'I've come out without my mackintosh and Mummy will be cross if I go home wet.'

'Yes, certainly,' said Mr Kindly. 'Take this one. I borrowed it from Mother Hannah. You can take it back to her tomorrow.'

Off went Little Corinne, the huge umbrella almost hiding her. Her mother was out when she got in, so she stood the umbrella in the hall-stand and went upstairs to take off her things.

Her brother ran down the stairs as she was about to go up. 'Hallo, Corinne! Is it raining? Blow, I'll have to take an umbrella, then!'

And, of course, he took Dame Lucky's, putting it up as soon as he got out of doors. Off he went, whistling in the rain, to his friend's house.

He put the umbrella in the hall-stand and went to find Jacko, his friend. Soon they were fitting together their railway lines, and when Pip said goodbye to Jacko he quite forgot about the umbrella because the sun was now shining again.

So there it stayed in Jacko's house all night. His Great-aunt Priscilla saw it there the next morning and was surprised because she hadn't seen it before. Nobody knew who owned it. What a peculiar thing!

Now, two days later, Dame Lucky put on her things to go out shopping and visiting. She looked up at the sky as she stepped out of her front door.

'Dear me—it looks like rain!' she said. 'I must take my umbrella.'

But it wasn't in the hall-stand. And it wasn't in the wardrobe in her bedroom, either. How strange! Where could it be?'

'I must have lent it to somebody,' said Dame Lucky. 'I've forgotten who, though. Oh dear, I do hope I haven't lost it for good!'

She set out to do her shopping. It didn't rain whilst she was at the market. 'Perhaps it won't rain at all,' thought Dame Lucky. 'I'll visit my old friend Priscilla on my way back.'

She met Jacko on the way. 'Is your Great-aunt Priscilla at home?' she asked him.

'Oh, yes,' said Jacko. 'She was only saying today that she wished she could see you. You go in and see her, Dame Lucky. You might just get there before the rain comes.'

She went on to the house where her friend Priscilla lived. She just got there before the rain fell. Dame Priscilla was very pleased to see her.

Soon they were sitting talking over cups of cocoa.

'Well, I must go,' said Dame Lucky at last. 'Oh dear —look at the rain! And I don't have an umbrella!'

'What! Have you lost yours?' asked Priscilla. 'How unlucky! Well, I'll lend you one.'

She took Dame Lucky to the hall-stand and Dame Lucky looked at the two or three umbrellas standing there. She gave a cry.

'Why! Where did *this* one come from? It's mine, I do declare! Look at the bird-handle! Priscilla, however did it come here?'

'Nobody knows,' said Dame Priscilla in astonishment. 'Is it really yours? Then *how* did it get here? It has been here for the last two days!'

'Waiting for me, then, I expect,' said Dame Lucky happily. 'Isn't that a bit of luck, Priscilla? I shan't need to borrow one from you. I'll just take my *own* umbrella! Goodbye!'

Off she went under the great yellow umbrella, very pleased to have it again. And whom should she meet on her way home but her brother, the very one who had given her the umbrella!

'Hallo, hallo!' he cried. 'I see you still have your umbrella! I *would* have been cross if you'd lost it. Let me share it with you!'

So they walked home together under the big yellow umbrella—and to this day Dame Lucky doesn't know how it came to be standing in Dame Priscilla's hall-stand, waiting for her.

He Wouldn't Take the Trouble

Oh-Dear, the Brownie, was cross.

'I ordered two new tyres for my old bicycle ages ago,' he said, 'and they haven't come yet! So I have to walk to the village and back each day, instead of riding. It's such a nuisance.'

'It won't hurt you,' said a friend Feefo. 'Don't make such a fuss, Oh-Dear! Everything is so much trouble to you, and you sigh and groan too much.'

Feefo was right. Oh-Dear did make a fuss about everything. If his chimney smoked and needed sweeping he almost cried with rage—though if he had had it swept as soon as it began to smoke, his rooms wouldn't have got so black.

If his hens didn't lay eggs as often as they should, he shouted angrily at them—but if only he had bothered to feed them properly at the right times, he would have got all the eggs he wanted.

Now he was angry because his new bicycle tyres hadn't come. It was really most annoying.

The next day he walked down into the village again to ask at the post-office if his tyres had come. But they hadn't. 'They might arrive by the next post,' said the little postmistress. 'If they do, I will send them by the carrier.'

'Pooh—you always say that—and they never do come!' said Oh-Dear rudely. He walked out of the shop. It was his day for going to see his old aunt Chuckle. He didn't like her very much because she laughed at him— but if he didn't go to see her she didn't send him the cakes and pies he liked so much.

Oh-Dear walked in at his aunt's gate. He didn't bother to shut it, so it banged to and fro in the wind and his aunt sent him out to latch it.

'You just don't take the trouble to do anything,' she said. 'You don't bother to shine your shoes each morning —just look at them—and you don't trouble to post the letters I give you to post—and you don't even take the trouble to say thank-you for my pies and cakes. You are so lazy, Oh-Dear!'

'Oh dear!' said Oh-Dear, sulking. 'Don't scold me again. You are always scolding me.'

'Well, you always need it,' said his aunt, and laughed at his sulking face. 'Now cheer up, Oh-Dear—I've a little bit of good news for you.'

'What is it?' said Oh-Dear.

'I've heard from my friend, Mr Give-a-Lot, and he is having a party tomorrow,' said Aunt Chuckle. 'He said that if you like to go, he will be very pleased. So go, Oh-Dear, because you love parties, and you know that Mr Give-a-Lot always has a lovely tea, and everyone goes away with a nice present.'

'Oh!' said Oh-Dear, pleased—but then his face grew gloomy. 'I can't go. It's too far to walk. No bus goes to Mr Give-a-Lot's—and I haven't got my new bicycle tyres so I can't ride there. Oh dear, oh dear, oh dear— isn't that just my luck?'

'Well—never mind,' said Aunt Chuckle. 'I should have thought you could walk there—but if it's too far, it's a pity. Cheer up. Look in the oven and you'll see a pie there.'

Oh-Dear stayed with his aunt till after tea. Then he set out to walk home. It was quite a long way. He groaned.

'Oh dear! It will be dark before I get home. Oh dear! What a pity I can't go to that party tomorrow. Oh dear, why isn't there a bus at this time to take me home?'

He went down the hill. A cart passed him and bumped over a hole in the road. Something fell out of the cart and rolled to the side of the road.

'Hi, hi!' shouted Oh-Dear, but the driver didn't hear him. 'Now look at that!' said Oh-Dear, crossly. 'I suppose I ought to carry the parcel down the road and catch the cart up—or take it to the police-station.'

He picked up the parcel. It was too dark to see the name and address on it, but it was very heavy and awkward to carry.

'I can't be bothered to go after the cart or carry this all the way to the police-station!' said Oh-Dear to him-self. 'I really can't.' And what's more I won't. Somebody else can have the trouble of taking it along!'

He threw the parcel down at the side of the road and went on his way. He wasn't going to take the trouble of finding out who it belonged to, or of handing it over safely. There the parcel lay all night, and all the next morning, for no one came by that way for a long time.

About three o'clock Cherry the pixie came along. She saw the parcel and picked it up. 'Oh!,' she said, 'This must have been dropped by the carrier's cart yesterday. Somebody didn't get their parcel. I wonder who it was.'

She looked at the name and address on it. 'Master Oh-Dear, the Pixie,' she read. 'Lemon Cottage, Breezy Corner. Oh, it must be the bicycle tyres that Oh-Dear has been expecting for so long. Well—the parcel is very heavy, but I'll carry it to him myself.'

So the kind little pixie took it along to Oh-Dear's cottage and gave it to him. 'I found it lying in the road,' she said. 'It must have dropped off the carrier's cart last night.'

'Yes, I saw it,' said Oh-Dear, 'but I wasn't going to be bothered to carry it all the way after the cart.'

'But Oh-Dear—it's for you,' said Cherry, in surprise. 'I suppose it was too dark for you to see the name on it. It's your very own parcel—I expect it's the tyres you wanted.'

'I found it lying in the road.'

'Gracious! It is!' said Oh-Dear, in excitement. 'Perhaps I can go to Mr Give-a-Lot's party after all.'

He tore off the paper and took off the lid of a big cardboard box. Inside were all the things he had ordered for his bicycle—two new tyres, a pump, a basket and a lamp.

Oh-Dear rushed to put them on his bicycle. He forgot to thank Cherry for her kindness. He worked hard at fitting on his tyres, but it was very very difficult.

At last he had them on—but when he looked at the clock, it was half-past six! Too late to go to the party now!

'Oh dear, isn't that just my bad luck!' wailed Oh-Dear. 'Why didn't you bring me the parcel earlier, Cherry?'

'Why didn't you take the trouble to see to it yourself last night, when you saw it in the road!' said Cherry. 'Bad luck, indeed—nothing of the sort. It's what you deserve! You won't bother yourself about anything, you just won't take the trouble—and now you've punished yourself, and a VERY GOOD THING TOO!'

She went out and banged the door. Oh-Dear sat down and cried. Why did he always have such bad luck, why, why, why?

Well, I could tell him the reason why, just as Cherry did, couldn't you?

Muddle's Mistake

There was once a brownie called Muddle. I expect you can guess why he had that name. He was always making muddles! He did make silly ones.

Once his mistress, the Princess of Toadstool Town, asked him to take a note to someone who lived in a fir tree. But Muddle came back saying that he couldn't find a tree with fur on at all!

Another time she asked him to get her a snapdragon and he said he didn't mind fetching a dragon, but he didn't want to get one that snapped.

So, you see, he was always making muddles. And one day he made a very big muddle. The Princess always said he would.

'You just don't use your eyes, Muddle,' she would say. 'You go through the world without looking hard at things, without listening well with your ears, without using your brains. You are a real muddler!'

Now once the Princess was asked to a party given by the Prince of Midnight Town. She was very excited.

'I shall go,' she told Muddle. 'You see, this prince gives really wonderful midnight parties, and he lights them by hanging glow-worms all over the place. It's really lovely!'

'Shall I go with you?' asked Muddle. I expect you will need someone to look after you on your way to the party, because it will be dark.'

'I think I shall fly there on a moth,' said the Princess. 'That will be nice. You get me a nice big moth, and you shall drive me.'

'Very well, Your Highness,' said Muddle, and he went off to get a moth. He hunted here and he hunted there, and at last he found a beautiful white-winged creature.

'Ah!' he said, 'just the right moth for the Princess. I must get it to come with me. I will put it into a beautiful cage, and feed it on sugar and honey, so that it will stay with me until the night of the party.'

So he spoke to the lovely creature. 'Will you come home with me White-Wings? I will give you sugar and honey. You shall stay with me until next week, when you may take the Princess of Toadstool Town to a party.'

'I should like that,' said White-Wings. 'I love parties. Get on my back, brownie and tell me which way to go to your home.'

Muddle was pleased. He got on to White-Wings' back, and they rose high in the air. It was fun. They were soon at Muddle's house, which was a sturdy little toadstool, with a little green door in the stalk, and windows in the head.

'Shall I put you in a cage, or just tie you up, White-Wings?' asked Muddle. White-Wings didn't want to be put into a cage. So Muddle took a length of spider thread and tied her up to his toadstool. He brought her honey, and she put out her long tongue and sucked it up. Muddle watched her.

'What a wonderful tongue you have!' he said. 'It is a bit like an elephant's trunk! I like the way you coil it up so neatly when you have finished your meal.'

'It is long because I like to put it deep down into flowers, and suck up the hidden nectar,' said White-Wings. 'Sometimes the flowers hide their nectar so deep that only a very long tongue like mine can reach it.'

Muddle told the Princess that he had found a very beautiful moth to take her to the midnight party. The Princess was pleased. 'Well, I am glad you haven't made a muddle about *that*!' she said. 'Bring White-Wings to me at twenty minutes to midnight and we will fly off. Make some reins of spider thread, and you shall drive.'

Muddle was so pleased to be going to the party too. It was a great treat for him. He had a new blue suit made, with silver buttons, and a blue cap with a silver knob at the top. He looked very grand.

When the night came, Muddle went out to White-Wings. The lovely insect was fast asleep. 'Wake up,' said Muddle. 'It is time to go to the party.'

White-Wings opened her eyes. She saw that it was quite dark. She shut her eyes again. 'Don't be silly Muddle,' she said. 'It is night-time. I am not going to fly in the dark.'

'Whatever do you mean?' asked Muddle in surprise. 'It is a midnight party! You *must* fly in the dark!'

'I never fly at night, never, never, never,' said White-Wings. 'Go away and let me sleep.'

'But moths always fly at night!' cried Muddle. 'I know a few fly in the day-time as well—but most of them fly at night. Come along, White-Wings. The Princess is waiting.'

'Muddle, what is all this talk about moths?' asked White-Wings in surprise. 'I am not a moth. I am a BUTTERFLY!'

Muddle lifted up his lantern and stared in the greatest surprise at White-Wings. 'A b-b-b-butterfly!' he stammered. 'Oh no—don't say that! No, no, say you are a moth!'

'Muddle, sometimes I think you are a very silly person,' said the butterfly crossly. 'Don't you know a butterfly from a moth? Have you lived all this time in the world, and seen hundreds of butterflies and moths, and never once noticed how different they are?'

'I thought you were a moth,' said Muddle, and he began to cry, because he knew that the Princess would be very angry with him. 'Please be a moth just for tonight and let me drive you to the midnight party.'

'No,' said White-Wings. 'I am a butterfly and I don't fly at night. If I were you, I'd go and find a moth now, and see if you can get one that will take you.'

'But how shall I know if I am talking to a moth or a butterfly?' said Muddle, still crying. 'I might make a mistake again.'

'Now listen,' said the butterfly. 'It is quite easy to tell which is which. Do you see the way I hold my wings? I put them neatly back to back, like this, so that I show only the underparts.'

The white butterfly put her wings back to back. 'Now,' she said, 'a moth never holds her wings like that. She puts them flat on her back—like this; or she wraps her body round with them—like this; or she just lets them droop—like this. But she certainly doesn't put them back to back.'

'I'll remember that,' said poor Muddle.

'Then,' said the butterfly, 'have a look at my body, will you, Muddle? Do you see how it is nipped in, in the middle? Well, you must have a look at the bodies of moths, and you will see that they are not nipped in, like mine. They are usually fat and thick.'

'I will be sure to look,' promised Muddle.

'And now here is a very important thing,' said the butterfly, waving her two feelers under Muddle's nose. 'A *most* important thing! Look at my feelers. What do you notice about them?'

'I see that they are thickened at the end,' said Muddle. 'They have a sort of knob there.'

'Quite right,' said White-Wings. 'Now, Muddle, just remember this—a moth *neve*r has a knob or a club at the end of his feelers, never! He may have feelers that are feathery, or feelers that are just threads—but he will never have knobs on them like mine. You can always tell a butterfly or moth at once, by just looking at their feelers.'

'Thank you, White-Wings,' said Muddle, feeling very small. 'All I knew was that butterflies flew in the day-time, and moths mostly flew at night. I didn't think of anything else.'

'Now go off at once and see if you can find a moth to take you and the Princess to the party,' said White-Wings. 'I'm sleepy.'

Well, off went poor Muddle. He looked here and he looked there. He came across a beautiful peacock butterfly, but he saw that it held its wings back to back as it rested, and that its feelers had thick ends. So he knew it wasn't a moth.

He found another white butterfly like White-Wings. He found a little blue butterfly, but its feelers had knobs on the end, so he knew that wasn't a moth, either.

Then he saw a pretty moth that shone yellow in the light of his lantern. It spread its wings flat. Its feelers were like threads, and had no knob at the tips. It *must* be a moth. It left the leaf it was resting on and fluttered round Muddle's head.

'Are you a moth?' asked Muddle.

'Of course!' said the moth. 'My name is Brimmy and I am a brimstone moth. Do you want me?'

'Oh *yes*!' said Muddle. 'Will you come with me at once, please, and let me drive you to the midnight party, with the Princess of Toadstool Town on your back?'

'Oh, I'd love that,' said the moth, and flew off with Muddle at once. The Princess was cross because they were late, and Muddle did not like to tell her why.

They went to the party and they had a lovely time. Muddle set White-Wings free the next day and gave her a little pot of honey to take away.

'You have taught me a lot,' he said. 'I shall use my eyes in future, White-Wings!'

Now let's have a game of Pretend! I am the Princess of Toadstool Town and you are just yourself. Please go out and see if you can find a moth to take me to a party! If you point out a butterfly to me instead, do you know what I shall call you?

I shall call you 'Muddle' of course!

Silky and the Snail

Silky was a pixie. She lived under a hawthorn hedge, and often talked to the birds and animals that passed by her house.

One day a big snail came crawling slowly by. Silky had never seen a snail, and at first she was quite afraid. Then she ran up to the snail, and touched his hard shell.

'How clever you are!' she said. 'You carry your house about with you! Why do you do that?'

'Well, you see,' said the snail, 'I have a very soft body that many birds and other creatures like to eat—so I grow a shell to protect it.'

'What a good idea,' said the pixie. 'Can you put your body right inside your shell, snail?'

'Watch me!' said the snail, and he curled his soft body up quickly into his shell. There was nothing of him to be seen except his spiral shell.

'Very clever,' said the pixie. 'Come out again, please, snail. I want to talk to you.'

The snail put his head out and then more of his body. He had four feelers on his head, and the pixie looked at them.

'Haven't you any eyes?' she said. 'I can't see your eyes, snail.'

'Oh, I keep them at the top of my longer pair of feelers,' said the snail. 'Can't you see them? Right at the top, pixie—little black things.'

'Oh yes, I can see there now,' said the pixie. 'What a funny place to keep your eyes, snail! Why do you keep them there?'

'Well, it's rather nice to have my eyes high up on feelers I can move about here and there,' said the snail. 'Wouldn't *you* like eyes on the ends of movable feelers, pixie? Think what a lot you could see!'

'I should be afraid that they would get hurt, if I had them at the end of feelers,' said Silky.

'Oh no!' said the snail, and he did such a funny thing. He rolled his eyes down inside his feelers, and the pixie stared in surprise.

'Oh, you can roll your eyes down your feelers, just as I pull the toe of my stocking inside out!' she said. 'Sometimes I put my hand inside my stocking, catch hold of the toe, and pull it down inside the stocking, to turn it inside out—and you do the same with your eyes!'

'Yes, I do,' said the snail. 'It's rather a good idea, don't you think so?'

'Oh, very good,' said Silky. 'Where's your mouth? Is that it, under your feelers?'

'Yes,' said the snail, and he opened it to show the pixie. She looked at it closely.

'Have you any teeth?' she said. 'I have a lot.'

'So have I,' said the snail 'I have about fourteen thousand.'

Silky stared. 'You shouldn't tell silly stories like that,' she said.

'I'm not telling silly stories,' said the snail. 'I'll show you my teeth."

He put out a long, narrow tongue, and Silky laughed. 'Don't tell me that you grow teeth on your *tongue*,' she said.

'Well, I do,' said the snail. 'Just look at my tongue, pixie. Can't you see the tiny teeth there, hundreds and hundreds of them?'

'Oh yes,' said the pixie in surprise. 'I can. They are so tiny, snail, and they all point backwards. It's like a tooth-ribbon, your tongue. How do you eat with your teeth?'

'I use my tongue like a file,' said the snail. 'I'll show you.'

He went to a lettuce, put out his tongue, and began to rasp away at a leaf. In a moment he had eaten quite a big piece.

'Well, you really *are* a strange creature,' said Silky. She looked closely at the snail, and noticed a strange little hole opening and shutting in the top of his neck.

'What's that slit for, in your neck?' she asked. 'And why does it keep opening and shutting?'

'Oh, that's my breathing-hole,' said the snail. 'Didn't you guess that? Every time that hole opens and shuts, I breathe.'

'Why don't you breathe with your mouth, as I do?' asked Silky.

'All soft-bodied creatures like myself, that have no bones at all, breathe through our bodies,' said the snail. 'Now, if you will excuse me, I must get into my shell. I can see the big thrush coming.'

He put his body back into his shell and stayed quite still. The thrush passed by without noticing him. The pixie went into her house, and came out with a tin of polish and a duster.

'Snail, I am going to polish up your shell for you,' she said. 'I shall make you look so nice. Everyone will say how beautiful you are!'

'Oh thank you,' said the snail, and he stayed quite still whilst Silky put polish on her cloth and then rubbed his shell hard.

'I rather like that,' he said.

'Well, come every day and I'll give you a good rubbing with my duster,' promised the pixie.

So, very soon, the two became good friends, and the snail always came by the pixie's house for a chat whenever he was near.

One day Silky was sad. She showed the snail a necklace of bright-blue beads—but it was broken, for the clasp was lost.

'I wanted to wear this at a party tomorrow,' said Silky. 'But I can't get anyone to mend it for me.'

'I know someone who will,' said the snail. 'He is a great friend of mine. He lives in a tiny house the fifth stone to the left of the old stone wall, and the fifteenth up. There's a hole there, and Mendy lives in it, doing all kinds of jobs for everyone.'

'I would never find the way,' said Silky. 'I know I'd get lost.'

'Well, I will take the necklace for you tonight,' said the snail. 'But I know Mendy will take a little time to do it, so you would have to fetch it yourself some time tomorrow.'

'But I should get lost!' said Silky.

'I will see that you don't,' said the snail. 'I will take the necklace to Mendy, give it to him, and come straight back here. And behind me I will leave a silvery trail for you to follow!'

'Oh, snail, you *are* kind and clever!' said Silky, delighted. She hung the beads over the snail's feelers, and he set off towards the old wall he knew so well. It was a long way for him to go, because he travelled very slowly.

It was a dry evening and the soft body of the snail did not get along as easily as on a wet night. So he sent out some slime to help his body along, and then he glided forwards more easily.

The slimy trail dried behind him, and left a beautiful silvery path, easy to see. The snail went up the wall to the hole where old Mendy the brownie lived, and gave him the broken necklace.

'It will be ready at noon tomorrow,' said Mendy. 'Thank you,' said the snail, and went home again, very slowly, leaving behind him a second silvery trail, running by the first.

Silky was asleep, so he didn't wake her, but he told her next morning that her necklace would be ready at noon.

'And you *can't* get lost,' he said, 'because I have left two silvery paths for you to follow. It doesn't matter which you walk on—either of them will lead you to Mendy.'

So Silky set off on one of the silvery paths, and it led her to the old wall, up it, and into Mendy's little house.

Her necklace was mended, so she put it on ready for the party. She was very pleased indeed.

'Thank you,' she said. 'Now I know the way to your house, I'll bring some other things for you to mend, Mendy!'

She went to find her friend, the snail. 'Thank you for leaving me such a lovely silvery path,' she said. 'I do think you are clever!'

I expect you would like to see the snail's silvery path too, wouldn't you? Well, go round your garden any summer's morning—you are sure to see the snail's night-time trail of silver gleaming in the sunshine here and there.

The Train That Went to Fairyland

Once, when Fred was playing with his railway train in the garden, a very strange thing happened.

Fred had just wound up his engine, fastened the carriages to it and sent them off on the lines, when he heard a small, high voice.

'That's it, look! That's what I was telling you about!'

Fred looked round in surprise. At first he saw no one, then, standing by a daisy, he saw a tiny fellow dressed in a railway guard's uniform, but he had little wings poking out from the back of his coat! He was talking to another tiny fellow, who was dressed like a porter. They were neither of them any taller than the nearest daisy.

'Hallo!' said Fred, in surprise. 'Who are you and what do you want?'

'Listen,' said the tiny guard. 'Will you lend us your train just for a little while, to go to Goblin Town and back? You see, the chief goblin is taking a train from Toadstool Town and our engine has broken down. We can't get enough magic in time to mend it—the chief goblin is getting awfully angry.'

'Lend you my train?' said Fred, in the greatest astonishment and delight. 'Of course I will, but you must promise me something first.'

'What?' asked the little guard.

'You must make me small and let *me* drive the train,' said Fred.

'All right,' said the guard. 'But you won't have an accident, will you?'

'Of course, not,' said Fred. 'I know how to drive my own train!'

'Shut your eyes and keep still a minute,' said the guard. Fred did as he was told, and the little guard sang out a string of very strange words. And when Fred opened his eyes again, what a surprise for him! He was as small as the tiny guard and porter.

'This is fun!' said Fred, getting into the cab. 'Come on. Will the engine run all right without lines, do you suppose?'

'Oh, we've got enough magic to make those as we go along,' said the little guard, and at once some lines spread before them running right down the garden to the hedge at the bottom. It was very strange and exciting.

'Well, off we go!' said Fred. 'I suppose the engine has only got to follow the lines, and it will be all right!'

He pulled down the little handle that started the train, and off they went! The guard and the porter had climbed into the cab of the engine too, so it seemed rather crowded. But nobody minded that, of course.

The lines spread before them in a most magical manner as the train ran over them, down the garden, through a hole in the hedge, and then goodness me, down a dark rabbit hole!

'Hallo, hallo!' said Fred in surprise. 'Wherever are we going?'

'It's all right,' said the little guard. 'This will take us to Toadstool Town. We come up at the other side of the hill.'

The engine ran through the winding rabbit holes, and once or twice met a rabbit who looked very scared indeed. Then it came up into the open air again, and there was Toadstool Town!

'I should have known it was without being told,' said Fred, who looked round him in delight as they passed tiny houses made out of the toadstools growing everywhere. 'Hallo, we're running into a station!'

So they were. It was Toadstool Station. Standing on another line was the train belonging to the little guard. The engine-driver and stoker were trying their hardest to rub enough magic into the wheels to start it, but it just wouldn't go!

On the platform was a fat, important-looking goblin, stamping up and down.

'Never heard of such a thing!' he kept saying, in a loud and angry voice. 'Never in my life! Keeping me waiting like this! Another minute and I'll turn the train into a caterpillar, and the driver and stoker into two leaves for it to feed on!'

'What a horrid fellow!' whispered Fred. The guard ran to the goblin and bowed low. 'Please, your Highness, we've got another train to take you home. Will you get in?'

'About time something was done!' said the goblin, crossly. 'I never heard of such a thing in my life, keeping me waiting like this!'

He got into one of the carriages. He had to get in through the roof, because the doors were only pretend ones that wouldn't open. The little guard slid the roof open and then shut it again over the angry goblin.

'Start up the train again quickly!' he cried. So Fred pulled down the handle again and the little clockwork train set off to Goblin Town. It passed through many little stations with strange names, and the little folk waiting there stared in the greatest surprise to see such an unusual train.

Fred was as proud and pleased as could be! He drove that engine as if he had driven engines all his life. He wished and wished he could make it whistle. But it only had a pretend whistle. Fred wished the funnel would smoke, too, but of course, it didn't!

Suddenly the train slowed down and stopped. 'Good gracious! What's the matter?' said the little guard, who was still in the engine-cab with Fred. 'Don't say your train is going to break down, too? The goblin certainly will turn us all into something unpleasant if it does!'

The goblin saw that the train had stopped. He slid back the roof of his carriage and popped his angry face out.

'What's the matter? Has this train broken down, too?'

Fred had jumped down from the cab and had gone to turn the key that wound up the engine. It had run down, and no wonder, for it had come a long, long way! It was surprising that it hadn't needed winding up before.

The goblin stared in astonishment at the key in Fred's hand. He had never seen a key to wind up an engine before. He got crosser than ever.

'What are you getting down from the engine for? Surely you are not going to pick flowers or do a bit of shopping? Get back at once!'

But Fred had had enough of the cross goblin. He slid the roof back so that the goblin couldn't open it again.

'Now you be quiet,' said Fred. 'The pixies and elves may be frightened of you, but *I'm* not! Here I've come along with my train to help you and all you do is to yell at me and be most impolite. I don't like you. I'll take you to Goblin Town with pleasure, and leave you there with even greater pleasure, but while we are on the way you will please keep quiet and behave.'

Well! The little guard and porter nearly fell out of the cab with horror and astonishment when they heard Fred speaking like that to the chief goblin! But Fred only grinned, and wound up the engine quickly.

There wasn't a sound from the goblin. Not a sound. He wasn't used to being spoken to like that. He thought Fred must be a great and mighty wizard to dare to speak so angrily to him. He was frightened. He sat in his roofed-in carriage and didn't say a word.

The train went on to Goblin Town and stopped. Fred got down, slid back the roof of the goblin's carriage and told him to get out.

The goblin climbed out quickly, looking quite scared.

'What do you say for being brought here in my train?' said Fred, catching hold of the goblin's arm tightly.

'Oh, th-th-thank you,' stammered the goblin.

'I should think so!' said Fred. 'I never heard of such a thing, not thanking anyone for a kindness. You go home and learn some manners, goblin.'

'Yes, yes, I will, thank you, sir,' said the chief goblin, and ran away as fast as he could. Everyone at the station stared in amazement.

'However did you dare to talk to him like that?' said the little guard in surprise. 'Do you know, that is the first time in his life he has ever said, 'Thank you'! What a wonderful boy you are!'

'Not at all,' said Fred, getting back into the engine-cab. 'That's the only way to talk to rude people. Didn't you know? Now then, back home we go, to my own garden!'

And back home they went, past all the funny little stations to Toadstool Town, down into the rabbit-burrows and out into the field, through the hedge and up the garden, back to where they started.

'Shut your eyes and we'll make you your own size again,' said the little guard. In a moment Fred was very large indeed and his train now looked very small to him!

'What would you like for a reward?' said the little guard. 'Shall I give your train a real whistle, and real smoke in its tunnel? Would you like that?'

'Rather!' said Fred. And from that very day his clockwork engine could whistle and smoke exactly like a real one.

The Golden Enchanter

Once upon a time there lived in Shining Palace a great enchanter. He had thick golden hair, a golden beard, and always dressed in tunics and cloaks made of cloth-of-gold. So he was known as the Golden Enchanter.

He was very, very rich. All his plates, dishes, and cups were made of the purest gold. The very chairs he sat upon were gold, and the table where he sat for his meals was made of such heavy gold that it could never be lifted.

In his cellars were sacks upon sacks of gold, but nobody ever saw them except the Enchanter, for only he had the key to those dark cellars.

Shining Palace was very beautiful. Its walls were built of gold, and there were very many windows, all shining and glittering in the sun that shone every day on the palace. The Enchanter loved the sun. He used its golden beams in his magic, and many a bright sunbeam he had imprisoned in his heavy bars of gold.

The Golden Enchanter was generous and kind-hearted. He gave much of his gold away, and the people loved him. But other enchanters were jealous of his riches.

The Green Magician who lived on the next hill envied him very much, and tried to learn his secrets. The

Hobbledy Wizard was jealous of him too, and wouldn't even speak to him when he met him. But the Golden Enchanter didn't mind. He felt sure that his gold was safe, locked up in the strong cellars.

One day there came to Shining Palace a little, lean man, whose eyes were a strange green. He asked to see the Enchanter and he was taken before him.

'Sir,' he said, bowing down to the ground, 'I have worked for Wily-One, the greatest of magicians, but he has turned me away after twenty years' service. So now I come to you to ask for work. There is not much that I do not know, for Wily-One was clever and taught me most of his secrets!'

'Wily-One was wicked,' said the Golden Enchanter sternly. 'I heard that he had been driven away.'

'That may be true,' said the green-eyed man. 'But listen to all the things I can do, O Enchanter, and I think you will find that I may be very useful to you.'

Then, in a long string, the lean man recited all the marvellous spells he could make, and, as he listened, the Enchanter's eyes opened wide.

'I do not know how it was that Wily-One the Magician trusted you so much as to tell you all the secret spells,' he said. 'Only enchanters are supposed to know them. Well, you must have proved yourself trustworthy to him, so I will engage you to help me. Start tomorrow.'

The green-eyed man bowed again, and a strange smile came over his face. The Golden Enchanter did not notice it or he would have wondered about it, and guessed the lean man's secret. For he was no other than Wily-One, the great magician, himself! He had been driven away from his castle, and had had to wander hungry and homeless about the country.

Then he had thought that he would disguise himself and go to the Golden Enchanter to beg for work. Once he was in the Shining Palace, surely he could steal the keys to the cellar and help himself to enough gold to make him rich again.

He was delighted when the Enchanter engaged him as his chief helper. Day after day he did magic for him, made strange spells, caught sunbeams for gold, and sang magic words as he stirred the big cauldron on the fire. But he could not get permission to go down into the cellars where the sacks of gold were kept. The Enchanter kept his keys guarded carefully, and slept with them under his pillow. He thought that his new servant was very clever, but he did not like him, nor trust him.

The green-eyed servant lived in a small cottage not far from the palace. One day he found a trap-door in the floor, and lifting it up, spied a small cellar underneath.

'I will keep my potatoes there,' he said to himself, and he went down the steps. But when he got there an idea came to him that made him shiver with delight.

'I will use my magic to bore a passage from this cellar to the cellars of Shining Palace,' he thought, and he set to work. All day long he worked for the Golden Enchanter, but half the night he worked for himself, bewitching a spade to dig deep into the earth, making a tunnel through the darkness.

At last the tunnel was finished. Wily-One crept through it and came to the small hole leading right into the cellars of Shining Palace. He was delighted. He was just about to crawl through when he heard the sound of

'He wanted to sneeze, but he dared not.'

footsteps. He crouched down in fear and saw that it was the Golden Enchanter himself, dragging a new sack of gold into place. As Wily-One hid behind the crumbling wall of earth, something tickled his nose. He wanted to sneeze, but he dared not. He held his nose tightly between his finger and thumb, and made the tiniest noise imaginable.

The Golden Enchanter had very quick ears, which could even hear the grass grow in the spring-time. He heard the tiny noise and wondered what it was. He thought it must be the click of a beetle's wings. He dragged the sack into place, and then went to another cellar.

Wily-One thought that he had better not try to steal any gold that night whilst the Enchanter was about. So, very quietly he turned and crept back along the dark tunnel to his cottage. He went to bed and dreamed all night long of the large sack of gold he would have on the morrow.

The Enchanter had a great deal of work to do the next day, for there was a very fine and delicate spell he was making. It was mostly made of cobwebs and the whiskers of gooseberries, and all the windows had to be shut in case the wind should blow in and upset the spell.

The green-eyed servant was helping. His eyes shone strangely and his cheeks were red with excitement. He kept thinking of that night, when he would once more have gold of his own and be rich. He would go far away to another country, build himself a fine castle, and be a magician once again.

The Golden Enchanter wondered why his assistant's eyes shone so green, and why his hands trembled when he carefully arranged the cobwebs in the right order.

'What's the matter with you this morning?' he asked. 'You don't seem yourself.'

'I'm all right!' said Wily-One.

'Now for goodness' sake don't sneeze or breathe too hard,' said the Enchanter, giving the last touches to the spell. 'If you do, all these cobwebs will have to be arranged again.'

But one of the gooseberry whiskers must have got up Wily-One's nose, for all of a sudden he wanted to sneeze.

He held his nose tightly between his finger and thumb and stopped the sneeze, making only the very tiniest noise, the same noise that he had made the night before in the cellar.

And the Golden Enchanter remembered the noise.

'So that's what that little noise was last night!' he thought to himself. 'It was this green-eyed servant of mine stopping a sneeze. It wasn't a beetle's wings clicking! Oho! I shall have to look into this. Perhaps this clever servant of mine is not what he seems.'

The more he thought about it, the more the Enchanter felt sure that his servant was really a magician—and suddenly he guessed Wily-One's secret! Of course—he was Wily-One himself, disguised! Wily-One had those strange green eyes too. However could he, the Golden Enchanter, have been tricked like this?

'I'll hide in the cellars tonight and see what he is up to,' thought the Enchanter. So that night very early he hid behind his sacks and waited. Just as he had guessed the green-eyed servant crept along the tunnel, climbed into the cellar, and caught up a sack of gold!

'Hi!' shouted the Golden Enchanter. 'Put that down you robber! I know who you are! You're Wily-One, the wicked magician who was driven away from his castle!'

Wily-One leapt through the hole and scuttled along the tunnel to his cottage. There he shut down the trapdoor and bolted it so that the Enchanter could not follow him. Then he took a magic broomstick he had once stolen from a witch, and rode away on it, taking the sack of gold with him.

But following him he saw a little bird, whom the Enchanter had ordered to chase Wily-One, for he did not like to leave his palace unguarded. He would call out his guards, bid them surround the palace whilst he was gone, and then follow the wicked magician himself. Meanwhile the little bird tracked Wily-One for him.

Wily-One landed at last in a broad field, so sleepy that he could fly no longer. Dawn was just breaking. He saw the little bird who had followed him wheel round and fly off towards Shining Palace.

'Well, by the time you come back with the Golden Enchanter I shall be gone!' he said. He looked at the sack of gold and decided that he had better bury it instead of taking it with him, for it was heavy. So he bewitched a strong stick and bade it make little holes all over the field. When that was done, he bade each piece of gold hide itself there. In a very short time the thousands of golden pieces were hidden all over the field, and there was none to be seen.

And at that moment Wily-One saw the Enchanter running towards him! He changed himself into a rabbit and ran away at top speed.

The Enchanter turned himself into a fox and a breath-less race began. Just as the rabbit was almost caught Wily-One changed himself into a lark. Up and up into the sky he rose, hoping to get away from the Enchanter.

But the Enchanter turned himself into an eagle and soared swiftly after the lark. Down the sky they went, the lark trying its hardest to escape. But with a downward rush the eagle was upon it, and both dropped to the earth. As they touched the ground Wily-One turned himself into a tiny mouse, hoping to hide among the bracken. But the Enchanter turned himself into a big black cat and began to hunt the mouse here and there. Smack! It clapped its great paw on to the mouse's back, and know-ing himself so nearly caught Wily-One changed swiftly into a snake and tried to bite the cat.

The Enchanter changed back into his own shape and struck the snake with a stick. It glided away and came to a deep pond. The Enchanter followed and lifted his stick again. Hey presto! Wily-One changed into a big fish and slipped silently into the water.

The Enchanter became an otter and slid into the water after him. Round and round the pond they swam, the fish twisting and turning in fear lest the otter should bite him in the neck.

Just as the otter pounced, the fish leapt into the air and changed into a brown bear. He clambered out of the water and ran to the mountains. The otter climbed out after him and changed into a bear too. He raced after his enemy, growling fiercely.

Wily-One saw a cave in a hillside and ran inside. In a trice the Golden Enchanter changed from a bear back to his own shape and laughed loudly. He took a great stone and rolled it in front of the cave, pinning it there by the most powerful magic he knew.

'Well, there you are, and there you may stay!' said he. 'I would never let a wicked magician like you free, for you do so much harm. No, here you will stay for hundreds of years and perhaps you will find time to repent.'

With that he left him and went back to Shining Palace. He did not bother to look for the stolen gold, for he had so much that he hardly missed it.

But one day he happened to pass the field where Wily-One had hidden the gold—and he stared in wonder and delight! Each little gold piece had taken root and grown! The plants had flowered in thousands all over the field and were waving their bright golden heads in the sunshine.

'I've never seen anything so beautiful in my life!' said the Enchanter. 'I hope the seeds will spread so that the flowers may be seen by everybody!'

They did spread—they spread all over the world, and now each summer-time you may see fields full of the bright gold flowers that once grew from the stolen gold. Do you know what we call them? Yes, buttercups, of course!

As for Wily-One, he is still in the cave, and long may he remain there!

Proud Little Dog

There was once a dog called Prince, and he lived with Dame Tiptap. She was very proud of him when he first came to her as a puppy, because his father and mother and his two grandmothers and two grandfathers had all won prizes.

Dame Tiptap gave Prince a beautiful basket of his own, lined with red flannel to keep him warm. She bought him a very expensive collar. She went to a pottery shop and had a special dish made for him, with his name 'Prince' round the bowl.

Prince thought himself very grand indeed. He looked at the old dog kennel out in the yard, and thought to himself, 'Ha! That may be good enough for ordinary dogs, but a dog like me sleeps by the fire, in a red-lined basket! I'm a prince among dogs!'

So, as he grew, he became very vain and proud. He looked down on the other dogs. He would not have a cat in the garden. He even chased away the birds that came for crumbs!

'Any crumbs in this garden belong to *me*!' said Prince.

'Fibber! They are put out for us!' chirruped the sparrow on the roof. 'Besides—what do *you* want with crumbs? Don't you have a big dinner?'

Prince did not like his mistress to have friends to the house. He growled at them. He even showed his teeth. Dame Tiptap did not like it.

She scolded him. 'This won't do, Prince. If you behave like that to my friends, I shall put you out into the kitchen when they come!'

'If you do a thing like that, I'll run away!' growled Prince, rudely.

'The trouble is, you're spoilt,' said Dame Tiptap. 'Now just you listen to me. Mistress Twinkle is coming to tea today. If you dare to bark or growl or show your teeth— out into the kitchen you go!'

Well, Prince *did* bark—and he did growl—and he did show his teeth! So out into the kitchen he went, and the door was shut firmly. He was very angry indeed, especially as he could smell muffins toasting in the sitting-room, and he liked them very much.

'I won't be treated like this!' growled Prince crossly. 'I shall run away! That will teach Dame Tiptap her manners. She'll miss me. She'll have no one to guard the house. Ha ha!'

He ran out of the back-door, down the path and away into the fields. He was a very good-looking dog, and he held up his head and kept his tail well up as he went. It was no wonder that a passing farmer looked at him closely and thought he would be a fine dog to steal!

'He's a valuable dog, anyone can see that,' said the farmer and he whistled to Prince. Prince ran up at once—

and the man slipped some rope through his collar and led him away.

'I'll tie him up for a few days and then sell him,' thought the farmer. 'Now come on, dog—don't drag behind like that.'

Poor Prince. He was taken to the farm-house and tied up tightly at the back. He was frightened and unhappy.

Dame Tiptap did not know where he had gone. 'Foolish dog!' she said. 'He has run away, as he said. Well, if he cares so little for his home and mistress, it is not much use worrying about him. Now I can have a cat of my own. I never dared to have one before. I'll tell Mistress Twinkle I will take the lovely black cat she has offered me—the one with eyes as green as cucumbers. She's a beauty, and will catch my mice for me.'

So the next day Green-Eyes came to live with kind Dame Tiptap. She settled down in Prince's basket by the fire, delighted to find such a good home. At night she hunted mice, and Dame Tiptap was very pleased with her.

Then somebody gave Dame Tiptap a canary in a cage to sing to her in the mornings. She hung it up in the window, and told Green-Eyes never to jump at the cage. It was lovely to hear the little bird singing every morning.

A week went by—and one morning, what a surprise for Dame Tiptap! In Green-Eyes' basket were four beautiful kittens.

'Well, well, look at that now!' said Dame TipTap, delighted. 'I've always loved kittens. Now we've got four! What fun we shall have when they run about!'

51

Now after some time Prince bit through the ropes that tied him, and ran home as fast as he could. He had had very little food. He had a cold. He was homesick and miserable. How he looked forward to his warm basket by the fire, a good dinner in the dish marked with his own name, and a great fussing from Dame TipTap! He ran through the back door and into the sitting-room, to find his basket and his mistress. But what was this? A big, green-eyed cat glared at him from a basketful of kittens, and then, with one leap, the cat was on Prince, and was scratching him with ten sharp claws!

'Woof, woof!' yelped Prince, and tore back to the kitchen. He heard the canary singing loudly in the window.

'Who's this bad dog, naughty dog? After him, Green-Eyes, after him! Trilla, trilla, trilla!'

Dame Tiptap went into the kitchen. 'So you have come back again, Prince!' she said. 'I thought you had run away and would never come back. You were so cross and bad-tempered because I had my friends here. I thought you would go to live with someone who was all alone. Surely you do not want to live with me again?'

'Woof, I do, I do, woof!' said poor Prince, feeling very sad and frightened. 'Let me have my lovely basket, and my beautiful dish, Mistress. I will be a good dog now.'

'I'm glad to hear that,' said Dame Tiptap. 'You can certainly live here if you wish, because it is your home. But your basket belongs to Green-Eyes now, and to her darling kittens, and Green-Eyes has your dish to feed from. But, if you like, you can have the kennel in the yard, and the old dish out of the scullery. Keep out of

52

So now Prince sometimes lies by the fire and warms himself.

the house, though, Prince, because if you don't I am sure Green-Eyes will fly at you!'

So poor Prince had to live in the yard and eat from the old scullery dish. He did not dare to go into the house. When he tried to, one cold afternoon, because he badly wanted a warm fire and a nice pat, Green-Eyes flew at him and scratched him all the way down his long nose.

'You keep out!' hissed Green-Eyes. 'This is *my* house, not yours! You belong to the yard. I don't like dogs. I'll let you live here if you keep to the yard. Mistress has got me and my four kittens, and a singing canary. She can easily do without a vain little dog like you!'

Prince knew that was true. He lost his pride and his bad temper. He grew used to the kennel in the yard. He gave Dame TipTap a great welcome whenever she came to see him. He greeted her friends with licks and yelps of joy.

'Quite a different dog!' said everyone. 'Perhaps when Green-Eyes' four kittens go to new homes she will make friends with him.'

The kittens went to new homes when they were eight weeks old. Green-Eyes no longer felt fierce and protective, anxious to save her kittens from a snapping dog.

Prince spoke to her humbly one day. 'It's very cold out here. Couldn't I come in for a few minutes? I won't lie in your basket.'

'All right. But mind—any nonsense and *out you go again*!'

So now Prince sometimes lies by the fire and warms himself, whilst Green-Eyes purrs in the basket nearby. Dame TipTap knits and smiles to herself. She thinks that

Prince will end up being quite a nice, sensible dog after all!

Prince lies there and stares at Green-Eyes—and he thinks to himself: 'It seems to me that Green-Eyes is mistress of this house now! Oh for the old days when Dame TipTap was mistress and I could do what I liked!'

But it was he himself who changed his good luck to bad, wasn't it?

She Turned Up Her Nose

In the nursery there lived a rather grand doll called Annabella Mary. She was dressed very well indeed in a blue silk frock, a hat with flowers in, shoes with blue bows on, and a very pretty white lace coat.

She thought herself a very grand person, and turned up her nose at all the other toys. She wouldn't join in their games. She wouldn't even have a ride in the little toy car.

One day the small dolls who lived in the dolls' house thought they would spring-clean it and make it beautifully clean and pretty. The children who belonged to the nursery were away, so it was a good chance to spring-clean the dolls' house.

'We'll all help,' said the rabbit. 'I'll scrub the floors.'

'I'll clean the windows,' said the Teddy.

'I'll beat the mats,' said Angela, the doll.

'I'll wash the curtains,' said the clockwork mouse. But it was a great pity the toys allowed him to do that, because he tore the lace curtains badly, and four of them couldn't possibly be put up again.

'Oh dear!' said the dolls' house dolls, sadly, looking at the great holes in four of their curtains. 'Oh dear! What a pity! The four bedroom windows will look awful now without any curtains. Never mind, don't cry, clockwork mouse—you did your best. It was our fault for letting a little thing like you wash the curtains.'

Soon the house was as clean and bright as a new pin. The floors shone. The carpets were beaten and put down again. The windows were clean. The fire-places had been swept out. The furniture had been polished, and the cushions beaten free of dust. Really, the house looked lovely.

'I think we ought to give a party to everyone,' said the dolls' house Mother-doll. 'They've been so kind in helping us to spring-clean.'

'We won't ask Annabella Mary, the doll,' said the dolls' house Father-doll. 'She hasn't helped at all. She just sat in her chair in a corner of the nursery, in her grand coat, and turned up her nose at us all working so busily at getting the house clean. We won't ask *her*!'

'Indeed we won't!' said all the others. So they didn't. Annabella Mary was the only toy who didn't get an invitation card to the party.

She didn't know anything about it until she saw the others reading their party-cards. She went over to the rabbit and peeped over his shoulder.

'Ha!' she said, pleased. 'An invitation to a party in the dolls' house! What fun! I love parties.'

'You're not going to be asked,' said the rabbit. 'You haven't got an invitation card have you? You see—you didn't help at all when we were so busy—so the dolls' house dolls didn't see why you should share in the fun afterwards. Quite right, too. You always turn your nose up at everything and everyone, so we are just as pleased you won't be going. You'd turn your nose up at the little cakes. You'd turn your nose up at the little cups of sweet lemonade. Oh it's a good thing you're not going.'

Now, it is a very horrid thing to be left out of anything nice, and Annabella Mary didn't like it at all. At first she was angry, and pretended to turn up her nose at the party. 'What a silly party it will be!' she said loudly. 'I'm sure *I* wouldn't want to go to it!'

But after a bit, when she saw how excited everyone was getting, and heard all about the little cakes and biscuits that were being made on the stove in the dolls' house, she felt very sad.

'Am I really so horrid?' she thought. 'Do I really turn my nose up at things and make people dislike me? It isn't nice not to be liked. I wish I'd helped to clean the dolls' house now. I could have taken off my grand coat and frock and worn an overall. I wish I hadn't been so mean. It serves me right to be left out!'

Annabella Mary felt sadder and sadder when the time drew near for the party. She stood by the dolls' house, and watched what was going on.

'I *do* wish the clockwork mouse hadn't torn the curtains for the four bedroom windows,' she heard the Mother-doll say with a sigh. 'The house looks so sweet—but the bedroom windows look empty and bare.'

Annabella Mary looked at the windows. They certainly did look bare without their little lace curtains. As she stared at them an idea came into her mind. What about her grand lace coat? Couldn't she cut it up into four bits, hem the ends, and make four little curtains for the windows?

'Oh, if only I could!' said Annabella Mary. 'That would show the toys I'm not so mean, after all. I'll do it!' So, whilst the others were all busy getting ready for the party, Annabella cut up the lace coat she was so proud of and sewed the four pieces neatly into little lace curtains. Then, much to the surprise of all the toys, she hung them up at the bedroom windows of the dolls' house. She was tall enough to reach the window without going inside the house. She opened each tiny window, and hung the curtain across.

'Look what Annabella Mary's doing!' cried the toys. 'Where did she get the lace?'

'Oh, she's cut up her beautiful lace coat, the one she's so proud of!' cried the rabbit. 'Annabella Mary, why did you do that?'

'Well, I hadn't done anything to help, you see,' said the big doll. 'And I suddenly thought of this. I've been mean and horrid, always turning up my nose—but now I feel different.'

'Oh Annabella, the curtains are SIMPLY LOVELY!' cried the dolls' house dolls. 'All they want is little bows of ribbon now!'

'Here they are!' cried Annabella, and snipped the blue bows off her shoes! She pinned them to the curtains—and, how fine the bedroom windows looked!

'You must come to the party, you really must,' said the rabbit. 'Why, you are a really nice person, after all. We shall have fun with you. Come and join the party. See if you like our cakes.'

So Annabella joined the party, and instead of turning up her nose at everything, and saying it wasn't nice, she said everything was lovely, and that it was the best party she had ever been to. It was, too, because, for the first time, she made real friends with everyone, and was as happy as could be.

The little bedroom curtains are still there, with tiny blue bows on them. I do wish you could see them!

The Snoozy Gnome

Have you heard of the Snoozy Gnome? His real name was Tippit, but he was always called Snoozy. He was the sleepiest, yawniest fellow that ever lived! He could go to sleep at any time—even whilst running to catch a bus!

Now one day Snoozy's village was tremendously excited. The Prince of Heyho was coming for the day, and so the gnomes decided to give a fancy dress party in his honour.

'It shall be at five o'clock in the afternoon, so that even the tiniest gnome can come,' said Mister Big-Nose, the chief gnome. 'Now all go home, please, and think out some really good fancy dresses for the party!'

Snoozy went home and sat down to think. 'I shall be a bear!' he decided excitedly. 'I can wear my bearskin rug, and pull the head right over my head. I will pin it tightly round me—and dear me, how astonished everyone will be! That will be a fine fancy dress!'

When the day came, Snoozy took up his bearskin rug and tried it on his back. He crawled about with the bear-head over his head, and the rug over his back. He really looked fine—just like a real bear!

'It's a bit big round my neck,' thought Snoozy. 'I must alter that. Let me see—what is the time? Oh, only two o'clock. I've got heaps of time till five.'

He got out a big needle and a strong thread and sat down to make the neck of the bearskin a little smaller. It was a hot afternoon and Snoozy rested his head against a soft cushion. He was very comfortable.

'Aaaaaah!' he yawned. 'My goodness, I'd like a nap. I do feel sleepy!'

He looked at the clock again. 'I think I'd have time just for 10 minutes' snooze,' he decided. 'Then I shall be all fresh for the party!'

So he lay back and fell asleep. The time went on— three o'clock, four o'clock, five o'clock! And still Snoozy slept on! He dreamed pleasant dreams. He was as warm as toast, and his armchair was very comfortable. Oh, what a lovely snooze!

Time went on—six o'clock, seven o'clock, eight o'clock, nine o'clock. Snoozy, aren't you *ever* going to wake up? The party is over—everyone has gone home and Mister Big-Nose is wondering why Snoozy didn't go to the party like everyone else!

Ten o'clock, eleven o'clock, midnight! Everywhere was quite dark and silent. Snoozy slept on, dreaming pleasantly. The clock ticked out the minutes in the darkness—but when the hands reached five minutes past four in the early morning, the clock stopped. It had to be wound up every night and as Snoozy had been asleep the evening before, it hadn't been wound up as usual.

After that there was no more ticking, and no more chiming! But the time went on—five o'clock, six o'clock, seven o'clock, eight o'clock! The sun was up, and most of the folk of the village. And at last Snoozy stirred in his armchair and stretched out his arms. He yawned widely—and opened his eyes. He looked round the room—and then he remembered the fancy dress party! My goodness!

'What's the time?' said Snoozy, and looked at the clock. 'Five minutes past four! Gracious goodness, and the party is at five! I must hurry. I have had a longer snooze than I meant to have. Dear, dear, now I *shall* have a rush!'

You see, Snoozy hadn't any idea at all that he had slept all the night through. He simply thought he had slept till five minutes past four the day before—and he thought it was yesterday, not today! Poor old Snoozy! He didn't think of looking at the sun to see whereabouts in the sky it was, for, like most sleepy-headed people, he was rather stupid—and though the sun shone in at the wrong window, he still thought it was the afternoon!

'I shan't have time to alter the bearskin now,' said Snoozy to himself. 'Can't be bothered! My, how hungry I am! I shall eat quite twenty cakes at the party, and I believe I could manage two or three jellies, and as for sausage-rolls, aha, give me fifteen of those, and you won't see them again!'

He put on the bearskin rug and pinned it tightly all round him. Then he pulled the bear-head over his own head, and pinned it well round his neck. He could hardly breathe, but he didn't mind. He was pleased to think he had such a fine fancy dress!

'Now, off we go!' said Snoozy and, crawling on all fours, he went out of his front door and down the street. As he went, he growled, because he thought that would make people look round and say: 'Oh, look! Here's someone in a wonderful fancy dress!'

But the party was over long ago—and the folk of the village were hurrying to do their morning shopping. When they saw the life-like bear walking down the street, growling, they were frightened.

'Oh, oh!' they cried. 'Look at that monster! He came out of Snoozy's house—he must have eaten him! Run, run!'

'Get a gun and shoot him!' cried Mister Big-Nose, meeting the bear round a corner, and getting the fright of his life.

Now Snoozy could NOT understand all this. So he stood up on his hind paws and shouted—or tried to shout through the bear head: 'I'm going to the party. Don't be frightened of me!'

But all that came out of the bear-head was something that sounded like: 'Ah-wah-wah-wah-wah-wah-wah! Wah-wah-wah-wah-wah-wah-wah! It was really very difficult to speak with a big bear-head over his face, and Snoozy tried his best to talk clearly.

'Oh! It's growling at us! It's a *fierce* bear!' shouted everyone in terror. 'Listen to it jabbering!'

Poor Snoozy was now quite puzzled. How stupid people were! Couldn't they even *guess* that it was a fancy dress? He shouted again, trying to say: 'I tell you, I'm going to the fancy dress party! Don't you UNDER-STAND?'

But all that came out was something like: 'Ah-who-wah, sh-wsh-wah-woo-wah-woowoowoo-wah! Wah-woo—YAH-HAY-YAH!'

'Oh! It's getting fiercer!' yelled the frightened people. Mister Big-Nose, fetch a gun! Oh, get a spear! Oh, where's a great big stick to knock it on the head! It'll eat us!'

Snoozy was now quite frightened. A gun! A spear! A stick to knock him on the head! Really, was everyone quite mad? Wasn't he telling them he was going to the party?

'I think I'd better go to the Town Hall, where the party is to be held, and then when people see me going up the steps, they will know I'm just someone in fancy dress,' said Snoozy to himself. So he dropped down on all fours again and padded off to the Town Hall. Behind him came crowds of people, talking, pointing, and all ready to run away at once if the bear so much as turned his head.

But he didn't. He went right on to the Town Hall. He padded up the steps and into the big hall where three gnomes were busily sweeping up all the mess from the party the day before.

Snoozy stopped and looked in astonishment. '*Where* was the party?' he wondered. 'No tea—no balloons—no people there—no nothing!'

He spoke to the three servants, who had been so busy with their work that they hadn't noticed the bear padding in. Snoozy said: 'Where is the PARTY?'

But all the three servants heard was: 'Wah-wah-wah-wah.'

'Ooooooh!' they screeched in fright, when they saw the bear. 'Ooooooh! A wild bear! Growling at us! Chase him out, chase him out!'

So, to Snoozy's great surprise and anger, the three little gnomes rushed at him and chased him out of the Town Hall! Yes, they really did, and it was very brave of them for they really and truly thought he was a wild bear from the woods.

'Don't! Don't!' yelled poor Snoozy. But as it sounded like 'Woof! Woof!' it didn't help him much.

Down the steps of the Town Hall went Snoozy. The three gnomes ran down after him and chased him into a very large puddle.

Snoozy was terribly upset. He sat in the puddle and cried loudly: 'Boo-hoo-hoo! Boo-hoo-hoo!'

And this time the noise he made was really like someone weeping, and all the villagers stopped and looked at one another.

'The bear is crying!' they said. 'The bear is crying! Poor thing! Perhaps he has come with a message to someone. Ask him, Big-Nose!'

So Mister Big-Nose stepped forward and spoke to the bear. 'Why have you come?' he said. 'Do you want to speak to someone?'

'No,' said Snoozy, and it sounded like 'Woof!'

Big-Nose shook his head. 'We can't understand what you say,' he said.

Just then a small, sharp-eyed gnome gave a shout and pointed to the bear's neck. 'He's got a safety-pin there!' he cried. 'Do you think it is hurting him?'

'Where?' said Big-Nose, astonished. When he saw the safety-pin, he was very sorry for the bear. 'Someone has put the pin there,' he said. 'Poor thing! Perhaps he came to ask us to get it out.'

'Where was the party?' he wondered.

He undid the pin—and to his enormous surprise, the bear's head dropped sideways, and out of it came Snoozy's own head, very hot, very rumpled, and with tears pouring down his cheeks!

'SNOOZY! It's SNOOZY!' cried everyone in the greatest astonishment. 'What *are* you doing in a bear-skin, Snoozy?'

'I c-c-came to the fancy dress p-p-party!' wept Snoozy. 'But I couldn't find it.'

But that was *yesterday*, Snoozy!' said Big-Nose. 'We wondered why you didn't come.'

'Yesterday!' said Snoozy. 'But I thought it was to be on Wednesday, not Tuesday.'

'Today is Thursday,' said Big-Nose. 'What have you been doing Snoozy? Have you been asleep or something —and slept all round the clock? This is Thursday morning. What did you think it was?'

'Why, I thought it was Wednesday afternoon! And I came out dressed in my bearskin rug to go to the party. And now I've missed the party. Oh, why did I take that snooze! I must have slept all the afternoon and all the night—and my clock stopped at five past four, and I thought that was the real time!'

Everyone began to laugh. It was really such a joke. 'Snoozy came to the party the day after!' said one gnome to another. 'Poor old Snoozy! What *will* he do next! Ho, ho! Perhaps he won't be quite so snoozy next time!'

Snoozy went home, carrying the bearskin over his shoulder. He was very unhappy. He got himself some bread and jam; for he was very hungry, and then he sat down to eat it. But so many tears ran down his nose into the jam that they made it taste quite salty, and he didn't enjoy his breakfast at all.

'That's the last time I snooze!' said the gnome. 'Never again!'

But it takes more than one lesson to cure a snoozer. Before a week was out, Snoozy was napping again— what a sleepy-head he is!

The Cat That Was Forgotten

Once there was a big black cat called Sootikin. He lived with the Jones family, and he killed all the mice that came to eat their crumbs.

Sootikin was a fine cat. His eyes were as green as cucumbers, and his whiskers were as white as snow. He was always purring, and he loved to be petted.

But the Jones family didn't pet him very much. Jane and Ronnie Jones were not very fond of animals, and Mrs Jones often shouted at him because he mewed round her feet when she was cooking fish.

Next door lived a boy called Billy. He loved Sootikin. He thought he was the finest cat in the world, and he was always looking out for him to stroke him.

'I wish Sootikin was mine, Mummy,' he said to his mother. 'I wish we had a cat.'

But his mother didn't like cats or dogs in the house, though she often said she liked Sootikin, and wished he would come and kill the mice in her larder.

Now one day the Jones family were very excited. They called over the fence to Billy.

'We're going away for a whole month to the seaside, to our Granny's. Aren't we lucky?'

'Yes,' said Billy, who had never even seen the sea. 'How I wish I was going with you!'

'We're catching the ten o'clock, train,' said Hilda. 'We'll send you a postcard.'

All the Jones family got into a taxi-cab at half-past nine and went off to the station. Billy felt lonely. He liked hearing the children next door shouting and laughing. Now for a whole month their house would be empty.

'I suppose they've taken dear old Sootikin too,' he thought.

But they hadn't, because, to Billy's great surprise, the big black cat suddenly sprang on to the top of the wall, and curled himself up in the sun. 'Mummy. The Joneses haven't taken Sootikin,' said Billy. 'Isn't that funny?'

Sootikin wondered where his family had gone.

71

'Oh, I expect they have arranged with a friend of theirs to come and feed him every day,' said Mummy. 'That is what people usually do when they have animals they leave behind. Maybe someone will come along with bread and milk or a bit of fish each day.'

Sootikin wondered where his family had gone. They hadn't even said good-bye to him. He went to the kitchen door after a bit and mewed to get in. But nobody opened the door. He went to see if he could find an open window, but they were all shut.

All that day Sootikin felt lonely, but he felt sure his family would come back in the evening. Then he could go indoors, have his milk, and jump into his own basket.

But his family didn't come back. Sootikin began to feel very hungry. There were no mice to catch, because he had caught them all. He wished he could have something to eat.

He had to sleep outside that night because he couldn't get into his house. It rained, and although Sootikin was under a bush, he got very wet. He sneezed.

He felt sad. His family had gone. They had forgotten him. They hadn't left him any food. They hadn't remembered that he had nowhere to sleep. They didn't love him at all. They were unkind.

He was very hungry the next day and the next. He found an old kipper bone and ate that. He chewed up an old crust.

When the fourth day came, he was thin and his coat looked rough and untidy. He had a cold. He didn't feel at all well, but he still felt hungry.

He thought of Billy, the boy next door. He had always been kind to him. Perhaps he would give him something to eat.

So Sootikin jumped over the wall to find Billy. He was in the garden, digging. Sootikin mewed.

Billy turned round. At first he hardly knew Sootikin, for the poor cat was so thin and his coat was no longer silky and smooth.

'Why—is it *you*, Sootikin!' cried Billy, and he bent down to stroke the cat. 'Poor, poor thing—you look so thin and hungry. Has no one been feeding you?'

Sootikin mewed to say that no one had fed him, he was lonely and sad, and please could he have something to eat.

Billy understood, and ran to his mother. 'Mummy,' he cried, 'poor old Sootikin is half-starved. Look at him—all skin and bone. Oh, Mummy, can I give him something to eat?'

'Poor creature!' said his mother, putting down a plate of fish scraps and milk. 'Here you are, Sootikin. He's got a cold too, Billy—he must have slept out in the rain at night.'

'Mummy, could he sleep in our kitchen till his cold is better?' said Billy. His mother nodded. She was kind and she didn't like to think that Sootikin had been forgotten like that.

Sootikin was glad. He ate a good meal and felt better. He washed himself and made his fur silkier. Then he jumped into a box that Billy had found for him, and went fast asleep.

He slept all night in the kitchen. He had a good meal the next day, and he slept the next night in the kitchen too—but not *all* night! No—he heard the mice in the larder, and he went to see what they were up to. Sootikin knew that mice were not allowed in larders.

Sootikin killed three big mice and one little one. He left them in a row to show Billy's mother what he had done. She was very pleased when she saw the mice.

'Mummy, that's Sootikin's way of saying thank you for our kindness,' said Billy, stroking the big cat, who purred loudly. 'Oh, Mummy, I do love Sootikin. I do wish he was my cat.'

'Well, the Joneses will want him as soon as they come back,' said his mother. 'You must make the most of him whilst they are away. I do think it was unkind of them to forget all about him like this.'

But do you know, when the Jones family came back, Sootikin wouldn't live with them any more. He simply wouldn't. Every time Billy put him over the wall, he came back again.

'He just won't live with us,' said Jane. 'Silly cat. He doesn't know his own home.'

'Well—you didn't seem to know your own cat—you forgot all about him,' said Billy. 'You don't deserve a cat like Sootikin. I hope he *does* live with us, and not you!'

Sootikin did. He had quite made up his mind about that. He never went into the Joneses' garden or house again but kept close to Billy.

'A cat can't help loving people who are kind,' purred Sootikin. 'I'm *your* cat now, Billy, and you're my little boy!'

The Dog Who Wanted a Home

There was once a dog who wanted a home. He had had a bad master, who was unkind to him, and he had run away because he was so unhappy.

'I shall find a new master, or perhaps a mistress,' said the dog to himself. 'I want someone who will love me. I want someone to love and to care for.'

But nobody seemed to want a dog, nobody at all. It was very sad. The dog ran here and he ran there, but either there was already a dog in the houses he went to, or the people there didn't want a dog.

He talked to his friend, the cat, about it. 'What am I to do?' he said. 'I must have a home. I cannot run about wild, with no food, and only the puddles to drink from.'

'Dogs and cats need homes,' said the cat, licking herself as she sat on top of the wall. 'I don't know of anyone who wants a dog. It's a pity you are not a cat.'

'Why?' asked the dog.

'Because I know a poor, blind old lady who badly wants a cat,' said the cat. 'She is lonely, and she wants a nice, cosy cat she can have in her lap.'

'Perhaps she would have a dog instead,' said the dog. 'If she is blind, I could help her, couldn't I? I could take her safely across the roads, and guard her house at night. A cat couldn't do that.'

'Well, she says she wants a cat, not a dog,' said the cat. Then she stopped licking herself and looked closely at the dog.

'I have an idea!' she said. 'You have a very silky coat for a dog, and a very long tail. I wonder whether you could *pretend* to be a cat!

'The poor old lady is blind and she wouldn't know.'

'I shouldn't like to deceive anyone,' said the dog.

'No, that wouldn't be nice,' said the cat. 'But after all, a dog *would* be better for the old lady, and when she got used to you, you could tell her you were a dog, and ask her to forgive you for pretending.'

'And by that time she might be so fond of me that she wouldn't mind keeping me!' said the dog joyfully. 'Yes—that is quite a good idea of yours, cat.'

'I will give you a few hints about cats,' said the cat. 'Don't bark, whatever you do, because, as you know, cats mew. If you bark you will give yourself away. And do try and purr a little.'

The dog tried—but what came from his throat was more of a growl than a purr. The cat laughed.

'That's really enough to make a cat laugh!' she said. 'Well, perhaps with a little practice you may get better. And another thing to remember is—put your claws in when you walk, so that you walk softly, like me, and don't make a clattering sound.'

The dog looked at his paws. The big, blunt claws stuck out, and he could not move them back into his paws, as the cat could. 'I must try to practise that too,' he said.

'Good-bye,' said the cat. 'I wish you luck. She is a dear old lady and will be very kind to you.'

The dog ran off to the old lady's house. She was sitting in her kitchen, knitting. The dog ran up to her, and pressed against her, as he had seen cats do. The old lady put down her hand and stroked him.

'So someone has sent me a cat!' she said. 'How kind! Puss, puss, puss, do you want some milk?'

She got up and put down a saucer of milk. The dog was pleased. He lapped it up noisily. 'Dear me, what a noise you make!' said the old lady in surprise. 'You must be a very hungry cat! Come on to my knee.'

The dog jumped up on to the old lady's knee. She stroked his silky coat, and felt his long tail. He tried his very best to purr. He made a very funny noise.

'You must have got a cold, Puss,' said the old lady. 'That's a funny purr you have! Now, go to sleep.'

The dog fell asleep. He liked being in the old lady's warm lap. He felt loved and happy. If only she went on thinking that he was a cat.

When he woke up, the old lady spoke to him. 'Puss, I want you to lie in the kitchen to-night and catch the mice that come. You will be very useful to me if you can do that.'

The dog was not good at catching mice. He was not quiet and sly like the cat. But he made up his mind to try. He did try, very hard, but as soon as he jumped up when he saw a mouse, the little animal heard his claws clattering on the floor, and fled away.

So in the morning there were no dead mice for the old lady to find. She was quite nice about it and stroked the dog gently.

'Never mind, Puss,' she said. 'You can try again to-night.'

The old lady was so kind and gentle that the dog longed with all his heart to catch mice for her, or to do anything to please her. He trotted after her all day long, as she went about her work. It was wonderful what she could do without being able to see.

'The only thing I can't do with safety is to go out and see my grand-children,' she told the dog. 'You see, I have to cross two roads to get to their house, and I am always afraid of being knocked over by something I can't see.'

The dog nearly said, 'Woof, woof, I will help you,' and just remembered in time that cats never bark.

The old lady was puzzled that day. Every time the dog ran across the floor she put her head on one side and listened.

'Your paws make such a noise,' she said. 'Surely you put your sharp claws in as you run, Puss? It sounds as if you are making quite a noise with them.'

So the dog was, because he couldn't help it. He couldn't put his claws in, like a cat. No dog can.

Then another thing puzzled the old lady. She put some milk on her finger for the dog to lick. The dog put out his pink tongue and licked the milk away.

'Well!' said the old lady, surprised. 'What a strange tongue you have, Puss! All the other cats have had very rough, scraping tongues but you have a very smooth one!'

'Oh dear!' thought the dog. 'This is quite true. Dogs have smooth tongues, and cats have rough ones. I remember an old cat licking me once, and I noticed how rough her tongue was—almost as if it was covered by tiny hooks!'

'I'll give you a nice meaty bone, Puss,' said the old lady at tea-time. 'You can scrape the meat off it with your tongue, and when you have taken away the meat, we will give the bone to the next-door dog to crunch. Cats cannot crunch bones, but dogs can!'

The dog was delighted to see the lovely, meaty bone. He lay down and began to lick it with his tongue, as cats do. But his tongue was not rough, and he could not get the meat off the bone.

It was sad. He was hungry and longed to crunch up the bone. He sniffed at it. He licked it again. Then he got it into his mouth and gave it a bite with his hard, strong dog's teeth, that were so different from the teeth of cats!

The bone made a noise as he crunched it up. The old lady was surprised. 'Well, I never heard a cat crunch up a big bone before!' she said. 'You must have strong teeth, Puss!'

She put on her hat and coat. 'I am going out,' she said. 'I shall try to get to the house where my grand-children live. Maybe someone will help me across the road. Keep house for me whilst I am gone, Puss.'

The dog did not like to see the blind old lady going out alone. He ran after her. When she came to the road she had to cross, he stood in front of her, making her wait until a bicycle had gone by. Then he gently tugged at her dress to show her that it was safe to go across.

The old lady was delighted. She bent down to stroke the dog. 'Puss, you are the cleverest cat in the world!' she said.

But dear me, when the old lady reached her grand-children safely, what a surprise for her! They ran out to greet her, all shouting the same thing.

'Granny! You've got a dog! Oh, what a nice one!'

And so at last the secret was out. 'No wonder I was so puzzled!' said the old lady, stooping to pat the dog. He barked a little, and licked her hand, wagging his tail hard.

'That's right!' said the old lady. 'Don't pretend to be a cat any more! Bark, and lick my hand and wag your tail! I'll have you instead of a cat. You're a kind little animal, and you'll help me across the road, won't you?'

'Woof, woof, woof!' said the dog joyfully, and ran off to tell the cat that he had found a home at last.

Freckles for a Thrush

An elf once came to the garden where the thrush lived. He was a clever little elf, and the thrush used to love to watch him at work.

He painted the tips of the daisy-petals bright crimson and spots on the ladybirds. He even painted the blackbird's beak a bright orange-gold for him in the spring.

The thrush was rather tiresome. He was always asking questions, always poking his beak here and there, always upsetting pots of paint.

The elf got angry with him. 'Look here, you big clumsy bird, don't come near me any more!' he said. 'I'm going to be very busy just now, painting mauve and green on the starling's feathers. If you keep disturbing me I shall get the colours wrong.'

But the thrush couldn't leave the little painter alone. He always had to peep and see what he was doing. Then one day he spied a worm just by the elf and darted at it. He pulled it up and upset half a dozen paint pots at once.

The colours all ran together on the grass, and the elf groaned.

'Look there! Half my colours wasted! That blue was for the blue-tit's cap—and that yellow was for the celandines in spring. I detest you, thrush. Go away!'

'I don't see why you should waste your lovely colours on stupid birds like the starling and the blue-tit,' said the thrush. ''They have nice feathers already. What about *me*? I am a dull brown bird with no colour at all, not even a bright beak! Won't you paint *me*, elfin painter—that would be a kind and sensible thing to do.'

'I don't want to be kind and sensible to you,' said the elf. 'I don't like you. Go away!'

'Yes, but elf, I do think you might spare me a little of your …' began the tiresome thrush again, and trod on the painter's biggest brush and broke it.

'*Now* look what you've done!' shouted the elf, in a rage, and he shook the brush he was using at the thrush. A shower of brown drops of paint flew all over the front of the surprised thrush, and stuck there.

'Oh—you've splashed my chest with your brown paint!' said the thrush crossly. 'I shall complain to the head-brownie in the wood. He will punish you!'

He flew off—but the head-brownie only laughed. 'It serves you right, anyhow!' he said. 'And why complain, thrush? Didn't you want your coat to be made brighter? Well, I think your freckled breast is very, very pretty. Go and look at yourself in the pond.'

The thrush went and looked into the water. Yes! He looked fine with his speckly, freckly breast. He liked it enormously. He flew back to thank the elfin painter, but he had collected his pots and gone off in a temper.

I like the freckles on the thrush, too. Do you? You might go and look at him. He's very proud of his freckles now.

He Didn't Want a Bath

'Tinker! Tinker! Where are you?' called Margery. 'I want to give you a bath.'

Tinker knew that quite well. As soon as he had seen the big wooden tub out on the grass he knew that he was to have that horrid thing, a bath!

Tinker hated baths. He hated having to stand in lukewarm water and be rubbed with soap and then scrubbed with a brush. He couldn't bear feeling himself wet and clean all over.

So he was lying under the bushes, very quietly indeed, hoping that Margery wouldn't see him.

'Tony—where's that dog gone?' called Margery to her brother. 'He *always* disappears at bath-time, always. He's really very annoying. I have everything ready, and the water's in the bath—but there's no dog.'

'There he is, under the bushes,' said Tony, pointing. 'I can see the end of his tail. He always forgets his tail when he hides!'

Margery saw the end of Tinker's tail. She crept up to it. She pounced—and Tinker sprang up. But it was too late. Margery had him by the collar now and was marching him to the bath.

Tinker whined. Margery had to get Tony to hold him in the water for her, because he struggled. She soaped him well, and he wriggled about till some went in his eyes. Then he howled dismally. Margery squeezed clear water over his head to get the soap out of his eyes.

He really was very naughty. He tried to jump out of the bath. He stood on the soap and went sideways into the soapy water with such a splash that he soaked Margery and Tony from head to foot.

'Tinker! You are being very, very silly. Look what you've done! Now stand still while I scrub you.'

He didn't stand still. He screwed this way and that way, and almost pulled Tony into the bath with him. And when at last he was rinsed and out on the grass he shook himself so violently that hundreds of silvery drops flew all over Margery and Tony, and even over Granny, who was sitting quite a long way off!

'Really! Tinker can be very naughty,' she said, wiping her skirt.

'Yes, he can. Tony, hold him while I try to dry him,' said poor Margery—but Tinker was off and away over the grass. He wasn't going to be dried! *He* was going to have a very good time indeed, now. He sniffed at himself. How horrid he smelt—all that nasty soap. What would the other dogs think when he met them?

They didn't like his smell at all. When he trotted up to Laddie, Laddie smelt him all over and then turned away in disgust.

'You don't smell like a *dog*,' he said, 'You smell disgusting. Go and roll in something nice and get that smell off!'

84

He Didn't Want a Bath

Tinker went to the field. He squeezed under the gate. There was a muddy patch by the stream where the cows stood. It always smelt very strong indeed. He would roll in that and then he would smell much better.

So he rolled in the mud, over and over. He looked very peculiar when he had finished. He was covered in patches of brown mud that smelt very strong.

He shook himself and went back to Laddie, 'Do I smell better now?' he said.

'A bit,' said Laddie. 'But I can still smell that soap. Look—rub yourself against that fence over there. It smells very strong indeed, but I don't know what of.'

A man had been painting the fence bright green and the paint was still wet. Tinker rubbed himself against it, first one side and then the other. Then he put his head over his shoulder and stared at himself doubtfully. He thought he looked a bit strange, with mud and now green paint. Also, he didn't like the smell of the paint after all. It made him feel sick.

Laddie didn't like it either. He sniffed at Tinker once more, looked disgusted and put his nose in the air. 'Horrible!' he said. 'Go and swim in the duck-pond, for goodness' sake, Tinker, and get that green stuff off!' Poor Tinker. He flung himself in the duck-pond and swam there. He got tangled in the weeds and came out with them twined round his head and legs. They smelt rather strong, too. But Laddie liked that smell better.

'That green stuff hasn't come off you,' he said, 'and I can still smell a bit of soap. But you do smell better now. I'll have a game.'

So they had a game, and by the time they had finished, Tinker's coat was dry—but, the patches of brown mud and the green paint made him look very strange—and the pond-water had left a very strong smell indeed.

'It's time to go home,' said Laddie. 'Goodbye.'

He went off to his home and Tinker trotted away to his. He went in at the front door and into the house. He was tired. He jumped up on to the sofa and lay down on the cushions there.

Mother found him. She tracked him by the terrible smell! She gave a shriek when she saw him. '*Tinker!* What *have* you been doing, you dreadful dog? You smell simply *frightful*! Margery! Tony! Come and take Tinker out of here at once. He needs a bath.'

Margery and Tony came running. 'Oh, you bad dog! Mother, he's just *had* a bath! Oh, you bad, naughty dog!'

They hauled him off. Margery went to get the tub. Tony went to get the water. Tinker went to hide in the bushes—and as usual he left his tail out.

And curiously enough, this story is going to end *exactly* as it began, which stories hardly ever do.

'Tinker! Tinker! Where are you?' called Margery. 'I want to give you a bath!'

He's a Horrid Dog

'There's a dear little puppy next door,' said Mummy to Alice. 'I saw him this morning. You'll love him, Alice.'

'I'll look out for him as I go to school,' said Alice. So she did, and she soon saw him, running round the next-door garden. The gate was shut, so he couldn't get out. Alice peeped over the top, and he rushed up and licked her on the nose.

'Don't,' said Alice, who didn't know that licking was a dog's way of kissing. She went off down the street, her satchel over her back, and her ball in her hand. She was not allowed to bounce it in the road, in case it went too near cars and she ran after it. She wanted to play with it at break.

Suddenly there came the sound of scampering feet, and after her tore the puppy! He had managed to jump over the gate, and wanted to catch her up. He had smelt the ball in her hand.

A ball. How that puppy loved a ball! His mistress often threw one for him, and he loved to scamper after it and get it into his mouth. A ball was the greatest fun in the world!

He jumped up at the surprised little girl. He knocked the ball right out of her hand! It went rolling along the pavement, and Alice gave a cry of alarm.

'Naughty dog! You'll make me lose my ball!'

The puppy pounced on it, threw it into the air, caught it again, and then danced all round Alice as if to say, 'Catch me if you can! I have your ball!'

But he wouldn't let Alice catch him, or get her ball, either. He ran off as soon as she tried to grab him. 'You're a horrid, horrid dog!' said Alice, almost in tears. 'I don't like you a bit. Give me my ball! You'll make me late for school.'

But the puppy was having such a lovely game that he couldn't possibly let Alice catch him. So, in the end, she had to go to school without her ball. She was late and the teacher scolded her.

'It wasn't my fault,' said Alice. 'It was the fault of the dog next door. He's a horrid dog. He took my ball away from me and wouldn't give it back.'

The puppy was waiting for her to come home, and as soon as he saw her he rushed out and put the ball at her feet. Really, he wanted her to play with him, and throw the ball for him to fetch. Alice wasn't doing that!

She picked up her ball and looked at it. The puppy had chewed it a little, and it wasn't such a nice-looking ball as before. Alice was very cross. She stamped her foot at the puppy and made him jump. 'Bad dog! Horrid dog! I don't like you! Go home!'

'Why, Alice!' said her mother's voice in surprise. 'I thought you'd love the puppy!'

'I don't. He's a horrid dog! I shan't play with him or take any notice of him at all,' said Alice. 'He's unkind and mean.'

And, do you know, she wouldn't pat him or talk to him, no matter how often he came rushing up to her. He was surprised and sad. Usually everyone made a fuss of him, for he really was a dear little fellow, with a tail that never stopped wagging.

Now, one afternoon Alice was going out to tea. She put on her best blue frock, socks and shoes, and a new hat with a blue ribbon round. It suited Alice beautifully.

'That's the prettiest hat you've ever had,' said Mummy, and kissed her goodbye. 'Hold it on tightly round the corner, because it's very windy today.'

Alice set off. The puppy came to meet her as usual, and as usual she took no notice of him at all. He trotted behind her, his tail down. What a funny little girl this was! Why didn't she give him a pat? The puppy couldn't understand it at all.

At the corner the wind blew very hard. Off went Alice's beautiful new hat. It flew into the road and rolled over and over and over, all the way back home. Alice gave a real squeal. 'Oh! My new hat! Oh, dear!'

The puppy saw the hat rolling along and he tore after it, barking. Was this a new game? Had the little girl thrown her hat for him to play with?

He was almost run over by a car. Then a bicycle just missed him. The hat rolled in and out of the traffic, and the puppy scampered after it. He caught the hat at last and was just going to toss it into the air and catch it again when he heard Alice's voice, 'Bring it here! Puppy, bring it here. It's my best hat!'

Ah! He knew the words 'bring it here!' He tore back to Alice at once and dropped the hat at her feet, his tail wagging hard. He looked up at the little girl with shining eyes and his pink tongue hung out of his mouth.

Alice picked up the hat. It wasn't damaged at all. She dusted it a little, and then put it on. She looked down at the puppy. 'Thank you,' she said. 'That was kind of you, especially as we weren't friends. But we will be now!'

'Woof!' said the puppy, and to Alice's surprise he put out his paw. Did he want to shake hands? He did! This was his newest trick and he was proud of it. Alice felt sure he was trying to say, 'Yes, we'll be friends! Shake hands!'

So they shook hands solemnly, and the puppy went all the way to her aunt's with Alice, waited for her, and then went all the way home. And she asked him in to play with her in her garden.

'But I thought you said he was a horrid dog?' said Mummy, in surprise.

'I made a mistake,' said Alice. 'I was the horrid one, Mummy—but now we're *both* nice!'

Hoppitty-Skip and Crawl-About

Hoppitty-skip was a frog. He could jump very high in the air, because his hind legs were long and strong.

One day he leapt high, and came down plop—but not on the ground! He had jumped on to the back of a toad!

'Crrr-oak!' said the toad crossly. 'Look where you are going!'

'Oh, I'm sorry,' said the frog, jumping off the toad's back quickly. 'You are so like a clod of earth that I didn't see you.'

'I suppose I am,' said the toad. 'It is a good idea to hide from enemies by looking exactly like the ground. Where are you going?'

'I am going to the pond,' said the frog. 'I think it is time I found a wife and had some eggs laid in the pond.'

'I shall soon be doing the same,' said the toad. 'I always go to the pond at the bottom of this field.'

'Oh, that's a long way away,' said the frog. 'I go to the little pond near by.'

'Don't go there this year,' said the toad. 'There are ducks on it.'

'Well, I will come to your pond, then,' said the frog.

'In a short time the frog had found a mate, and she had laid her eggs in a big mass of jelly in the pond. The toad, too, had eggs, but they were not in a mass—they were in a doublestring of jelly, wound in and out of the water-weeds.

'My eggs rise up to the surface where the sun can warm them,' said the frog. 'Look—you can see the tiny black specks wriggling in the jelly. They are tadpoles already.'

Soon there were both frog and toad tadpoles in the pond. They wriggled about and had a lovely time.

'Let us leave the pond now,' said the frog to the toad. 'I am tired of all these wriggling tadpoles. We will go and find a nice damp place somewhere in a ditch.'

So they left the warm pond and made their way to a ditch the toad knew. The frog went by leaps and bounds, but the toad didn't. He either crawled, or did some funny little hops that made the frog laugh.

'Why don't you leap along like me?' he said. 'You're so slow.'

'I am not made like you,' said the toad. 'I am heavier and my legs are shorter. Anyway, why do you leap along so quickly? It is a hot day. Go slowly.'

'I can't help jumping,' said the frog. 'And besides, Crawl-About, my high leaps are very useful to me some-times, when enemies are near.'

'I don't believe it,' said Crawl-About. 'It is much wiser to crouch on the ground and pretend to be a clod of earth, as I do.'

Just then a rat came by and saw the frog and the toad. The toad sank to the earth and seemed to vanish, he was so like the soil. The rat pounced on the frog—but at once the little creature rose high in the air, and the rat ran back, startled. By the time he had come back again to find the frog, Hoppitty-Skip had vanished into some long grass.

He waited until the rat had gone. Then he looked for his friend. He could not see him at all—and then suddenly he saw the toad's beautiful coppery eyes looking at him near by. He was still crouching on the ground, so like it that the frog could only make out his shining eyes.

'Well, did you see how I startled the rat?' asked the frog in delight. 'Didn't I make him jump? I just had time to vanish into the long grass.'

'Well, your way of dealing with enemies is good for you, and mine is good for me,' said the toad, beginning to crawl again. 'We all have our different ways, Hoppitty-Skip. Mine is to crouch down and keep still, yours is to jump. I have another way of getting the better of an enemy too.'

'What's that?' asked the frog. But the toad had no breath to tell him.

They found a good place in a ditch. The long grass was damp there, and both the creatures liked that. They did not like dryness. They sat and waited for food to come to them. The toad fell asleep.

The frog had a lovely time. A big bluebottle fly came along and perched on a leaf just above the frog's head. Out flicked his tongue—and the fly was gone! The frog blinked his eyes and swallowed.

He waited for another fly to come. But the next thing that came along was a fat green caterpillar, arching its back as it crawled.

Out flicked the frog's tongue—and the surprised caterpillar disappeared down the frog's throat.

'I say!' said a little mouse near by. 'I say, Hoppitty-Skip—how do you manage to catch flies and grubs so easily? You must have a very long tongue!'

'I've a very clever sort of tongue,' said the frog, and he flicked it out to show the mouse. 'Look, it's fastened to the front of my mouth, instead of the back, as yours is. So I can flick it out much farther!'

He flicked it out again and hit the mouse on the nose with it. 'Don't,' said the mouse. 'Your tongue feels sticky. Look—there's another fly!'

A big fly was buzzing just above their heads. The frog flicked out his long tongue, and flicked it back again. The fly was stuck on the end of his tongue, and went down his throat! 'Most delicious,' said the frog. 'It's a very great pity old Crawl-About sleeps all the day—he misses such a lot of good meals!'

Crawl-About woke up at night. He gave a croak and set out on a walk. 'Where are you going?' called the frog, who wanted to sleep. 'You'll lose your way in the dark.'

'No, I shan't,' said the toad. 'I never do. I always know my way back easily. I am off to find a few slugs, a score or so of beetles, and maybe even a baby mouse if I can get one. I'll be back by the morning.'

Sure enough, he was back in his place by the morning, though he had crawled and hopped quite a long way in the night. He told Hoppitty-Skip that he had had a very good time, and eaten so many things that all he wanted to do now was to sleep.

'You must have a very long tongue.'

'You are not really very good company,' said the frog. 'You like to sleep all day and wander off at night. Well, well—all the more flies for me, I suppose!'

The frog's body was smooth and fresh-looking. The toad's was pimply and dark, much drier than the frog's. The frog thought he had much the nicer body of the two, and he was glad he had quick legs and a high bound. It was fun to be in the field in that hot summer weather. It was always moist in the ditch.

One day the rat came back again. The frog gave a great leap and got away. The toad crouched down flat as before. But the rat saw him and pounced fiercely on him.

'Now he'll be eaten!' said Hoppitty-Skip, in fright. 'Oh, what a pity he hasn't a good high jump as I have, then he could get away quickly.'

But the toad had yet another way in which he could get rid of an enemy. From his pimply body he sent out some nasty-smelling, nasty-tasting stuff. The rat got a taste of it and drew back, his mouth open in disgust.

'Eat me if you like,' croaked the toad, 'but I shall be the most horrible-tasting meal you have ever had! I may even poison you. Lick me, rat—taste me! Do you still think you would like me for a meal?'

The rat fled, still with his mouth wide open. He couldn't bear the horrible taste on his tongue. Oh, he would never, never pounce on a toad again!

'Are you there, Hoppitty-Skip?' asked Crawl-About. 'Don't look so frightened. I am quite all right. Your trick of leaping is very good—but my trick of hiding, and of sending out nasty-tasting stuff all over my back, is even better!'

Soon the cold days came. 'I must get back to the pond,' said the frog. 'Come with me, Crawl-About. Come and sleep in the mud with me. We shall be safe there all through the winter.'

'I might,' said the toad sleepily. 'Go and have a look at the pond and see if it is very crowded.'

The frog went, and soon came hopping back. The toad was under a big stone. The frog peeped beneath it.

'Come to the pond,' he said. 'There is plenty of room. I have found two good places in the mud at the bottom.'

But there was no answer. The toad had already gone to sleep for the winter! Nothing would wake him. He slept soundly under his stone, looking like a dark piece of earth.

'Well, there's no waking him,' said Hoppitty-Skip. 'Good-bye, Crawl-About. I'm off to sleep in the pond. See you again in the spring!'

And off he hopped to sleep the cold days and nights away, tucked into the mud at the bottom of the pond. You won't be able to see him in the winter—but you might find Crawl-About. Don't disturb him, will you.

The Lamb Without a Mother

Ellen was staying at her uncle's farm. She liked being there, because there were so many nice things to do. She could feed the hens. She could take milk in a pail to the new calf. She could ride on Blackie, the old farm-horse.

It was winter-time, so it was not such fun as in the summer-time. But there was one great excitement—and that was the coming of the new lambs!

Ellen loved the baby lambs. The old shepherd lived in his hut on the hillside near the sheep, so that he could look after them when their lambs were born. Ellen often used to go and talk to him.

'Ah, it's a busy time with me,' said the old shepherd. 'Sometimes many lambs are born the same night, and there are many babies to see to. You come and look at these two—a sweet pair they are!'

Ellen peeped into a little fold and saw a big mother-sheep there, with two tiny lambs beside her. Each of them had black noses, and they were butting them against their mother.

'I love them,' said Ellen. 'What do you feed them on, shepherd?'

'Oh, the mother feeds them,' said the shepherd with a laugh. 'Didn't you know, missy? Ah, yes, the lambs suck their mother's milk, and that's what makes them frisky and strong.'

'What a good idea,' said Ellen, and she watched the tiny lambs drinking their mother's milk. 'Aren't they hungry, shepherd!'

'Little creatures always are,' said the shepherd. 'They have to grow big, you see, so they want a lot of food to build up their growing bodies. Birds bring grubs to their little ones, caterpillars eat the leaves of plants, young fish find their own food—and lambs drink their mother's milk.'

One day, when Ellen went to see the old shepherd, she found him looking sad. 'One of the mother-sheep has died' he said. 'And she has left this little lamb behind her.'

'Oh dear—and it has no mother to get milk from!' said Ellen sadly. 'Will it die too?'

'I am going to see if another mother-sheep will take it,' said the shepherd. 'Maybe she will. She has only one lamb.'

So he gave the tiny lamb to another sheep. But she butted it away angrily.

'Isn't she unkind?' said Ellen, almost in tears. 'She's got one lamb of her own, and surely she wouldn't mind having another. Most of the sheep have two.'

'She isn't really unkind,' said the shepherd. 'She doesn't know the strange smell of this little lamb, so she doesn't like it. Well, well—she won't have it, that's plain!'

'What will you do?' asked Ellen.

'It will have to be fed from a baby's bottle,' said the shepherd. 'I shall put milk into a bottle, put a teat on it, and let the lamb suck. Then it will live.'

Ellen stared at him in surprise. 'Can you really feed a lamb out of a baby's bottle?' she said. 'Oh, shepherd, please may I watch you?'

'Of course,' said the shepherd. He took out a glass bottle from his shed. He washed it, and then put some warm milk into it. He fitted a large teat on the end, and went to where he had left the tiny lamb.

He smeared the teat with milk and pushed it against the lamb's black nose. The tiny creature sniffed at it and then put out its tongue and licked it.

'It likes the taste!' said Ellen in excitement. 'Oh, lamb, do drink the milk!'

The lamb opened his mouth and took hold of the milky teat. He sucked—for that is a thing that all lambs, all calves, all babies know how to do. He sucked hard.

The milk came through the teat and went into his mouth. The lamb sucked and sucked. He was hungry. The milk was nice. He sucked until he had nearly finished the bottle.

Ellen watched him in delight. 'Please, please do let me hold the bottle whilst he finishes the few last drops,' she begged the shepherd. So he gave her the bottle to hold.

Ellen loved feeding the tiny lamb. She liked feeling him pulling hard at the bottle. He finished every drop of the milk, and licked the teat. Then he gave a sigh of happiness, as if to say, 'That was really nice!'

'He'll do all right,' said the shepherd, taking the empty bottle. 'The pity is—I've no time to bottle-feed lambs just now.'

'Shepherd—let me do it, then!' cried Ellen. ' I know Uncle will let me. Can I go and ask him?'

The tiny creature sniffed at it.

The shepherd nodded, and Ellen sped off down the hill to where her uncle was working in the fields.

'Uncle! There's a lamb without a mother, so it hasn't any mother's milk to drink! The shepherd says it must be fed from a baby's bottle. Can I feed it for him every day, please, Uncle?'

'If you like,' said her uncle. 'It will need to be fed many times a day, Ellen, so you mustn't forget. You had better let the shepherd bring it down into the farmhouse garden for you. It can live there, and you can easily feed it from a bottle then, without climbing the hill every time.'

Ellen ran to tell the shepherd. 'You needn't carry it down for me,' she said. 'I can carry the little thing myself.'

So she carried the little warm creature down to the garden. She shut the gate carefully so that it could not get out. It seemed to like being there, and frisked round happily.

Ellen fed it when it was hungry. Her aunt put milk into the baby's bottle, and Ellen went to take it to the lamb. He soon knew her and ran to meet her. How he sucked the milk from the bottle! He almost pulled it out of Ellen's hand sometimes!

He grew well. He had a tight, woolly coat to keep him warm, and a long wriggling tail. He could jump and spring about cleverly. Ellen often played with him in the garden, and they loved one another very much.

He grew quite fat and tubby. Ellen looked at him one day and said, 'You are almost like a little sheep. Don't grow into a sheep, little lamb. Sheep never play. They just eat grass all day long, and say "Baa-baa-baa".'

The Lamb Without a Mother

The lamb could bleat in his little high voice. Some-times he would bleat for Ellen to bring him a bottle of milk. 'Maa-maaa-maa!' he would say.

But soon there came a time when he did not need to drink milk any more. He could eat grass. He nibbled at it and liked it. Ellen watched him eating it, and was afraid that soon he would have to leave the garden and go into the big field with the others.

'Then you will forget about me, and won't come running to meet me any more,' she said sadly.

One day the big sheep were sheared. The farmyard was full of their bleating, for they did not like their warm, thick woolly coats being cut away from them.

Ellen watched the shearing. 'What a lot of wool!' she said. I suppose that will be washed, and woven, and made into warm clothes. How useful the sheep are to us.'

The lamb was not sheared. He was allowed to keep his coat that year. 'It is not thick enough for shearing,' said the shepherd. 'The lambs keep their coats. They will be very thick next year. And now, I think your lamb must come and live in the field. He is old enough to be with the others, now that you have quite finished feeding him by bottle.'

Ellen was sad. She took the little lamb from the farmhouse garden to the field. She opened the gate and let him through. He stood quite still and stared at all the sheep and lambs there.

Then a small lamb came up to him. 'Come and play "Jump-high, jump-low" with us,' he said. 'It's such fun.'

The little lamb frisked off in delight. 'He has forgotten me already,' said Ellen.

But he hadn't. Whenever the little girl goes by the field, the lamb comes running up to the hedge, bleating. He pushes his nose through, and Ellen pats him. And I expect that he will always remember his little friend, and run happily to greet her, don't you?

Moo-ooo-ooo!

Once upon a time there was a little girl called Lucy. She lived in a big town, and every year she went to the seaside.

But one year she went to stay in the country instead. Her mother sent her to stay with her Aunt Mary on a big farm.

'You will have such a lovely time, Lucy,' said her mother. 'You will have chickens and ducks round you, big sheep in the fields, and perhaps Aunt Mary will let you ride on one of the big horses.'

'Will there be cows?' asked Lucy.

'Oh yes,' said her mother. 'Lovely big red and white cows that say "Mooo-ooo-ooo!" You will like them, Lucy.'

'I shan't,' said Lucy. 'I'm afraid of cows.'

'Silly girl,' said her mother. 'There's no need to be afraid of cows. They won't hurt you.'

'They might toss me with their big horns,' said Lucy

'Of course they won't,' said her mother. 'Cows are gentle animals. You will like them.'

But Lucy didn't like them. As soon as she was down at the farm, she began to look out for cows. She saw some in a field—and oh dear, as she walked by the field, one of the cows put its head over the hedge and mooed loudly.

'Mooo-ooo-ooo!' it said. It did make poor Lucy jump. She ran home crying, and her aunt was sorry.

'Darling, the cows won't hurt you,' she said. 'They are our friends. They give us lots of nice things, really they do.'

'They don't give *me* anything,' sobbed Lucy. 'At least, they only give me nasty things. That cow gave me a horrid fright.'

'Well, come with me and feed the hens,' said Aunt Mary. Lucy dried her eyes and went with her aunt.

When she came back again it was eleven o'clock. Her aunt went to the larder and brought out a bun. Then she poured some rich yellow milk into a blue cup.

'A present from the cow,' she said to Lucy. 'Drink it up and see how nice it is. The cow gave it to me this morning, and I put it in a jug for you.'

Lucy tasted the milk. It was simply lovely. 'It's much nicer than my milk at home,' she said. 'Did the cow really give it to me?'

'Yes, it came from the cow,' said Aunt Mary. 'As soon as you stop being afraid of my dear old cows, I want you to come with me and see me milk them. You will like to hear the milk splashing into the pail. It is a lovely sound.'

When dinner-time came, there was an apple pie for pudding. Lucy was glad.

'It's one of my favourite puddings,' she said. 'Is there any custard, Auntie?'

'No,' said her aunt. 'But the cow sent you this instead. You will like it.'

Moo-ooo-ooo!

Aunt Mary put a little blue jug of cream down beside Lucy's plate. 'Pour it out over your pie yourself,' she said. 'It is all for you. Have it all and enjoy it. Isn't the cow kind?'

Lucy poured out the cream over her pie. It was thick and yellow and tasted very good.

In the afternoon she went out to play, but she didn't go near the field where the cows were. 'If I do they will shout "Moo-ooo-ooo" at me again,' she said to herself.

When tea-time came Lucy was hungry. She was glad to hear the tea-bell and ran indoors. There was a loaf of crusty new bread on the table, and beside it was a white dish full of golden-yellow butter. There was a pot of strawberry jam, and some buns. Lucy thought it was a lovely tea.

'What lovely golden butter!' she said. 'Can I spread it on my piece of bread myself Auntie? Mother lets me at home.'

'Yes, you can,' said Aunt Mary. 'It's a present from the cow again.'

'*Is* it?' said Lucy, surprised. 'I didn't know butter came from the cow.'

'Well, we make it from the cream that we get from the milk that the cow gives us,' said Aunt Mary. 'So it is really a present from the cow, too, you see.'

'Oh,' said Lucy, spreading her bread with the rich yellow butter. 'The cow *does* give us a lot of things, doesn't it?'

Lucy met the cows that evening as they walked to their milking-place. One mooed rather loudly and she ran away again. She told her aunt about it at supper-time.

'That nasty horrid cow mooed loudly at me again,' she said. 'I don't like cows. They are horrid things.'

'Dear me, I'm sorry,' said Aunt Mary, as she set down Lucy's supper in front of her. 'I suppose you won't want to eat another present from the cow, then?'

'Does this lovely cheese come from the cow too?' cried Lucy, in great surprise. 'Oh, Aunt Mary—I didn't know that! Milk—and cream and butter—and cheese! Well, really, what a nice animal!'

Lucy ate her bread and butter and cheese. She had some stewed apple and cream, and she drank a glass of milk. What a number of things came from the cow! She thought about it quite a lot.

'Auntie,' she said the next day, 'I think I am wrong to be silly about cows. But I can't help it. Do you think if I got used to baby cows first, I would grow to like grown-up cows?'

'I am sure you would,' said Aunt Mary. 'That is a very good idea! We have some calves, and you shall help me to feed them today. You shall see me feed a little new-born calf. You will like that.'

'Do calves grow into cows?' asked Lucy, trotting after her aunt.

'Oh yes, always,' said Aunt Mary. 'Now look, here is our very youngest baby. We must teach her to suck milk. We cannot let her suck her mother's milk—that big cow over there—because we want all *her* milk to sell; so we must feed her out of a pail.'

The baby calf was very sweet. She was rather wobbly on her long legs, and she had the softest brown eyes that Lucy had ever seen. She sniffed at Lucy's hand and then began to suck it.

'Oh—she's very hungry, Auntie,' said Lucy. 'She's trying to suck my hand.'

It wasn't long before Aunt Mary had a pail of milk ready for the calf. 'Now watch me teach her to drink,' she said.

She dipped her fingers in the milk and held them out to the calf. The calf sniffed the milk and then licked it eagerly, trying to take Aunt Mary's hand into her mouth. She dipped her fingers in the pail of milk again, and once more the calf licked the milk off.

The next time Aunt Mary did not hold her fingers out so far. She held them in the pail. The calf put her head in the pail, and followed her fingers down. Aunt Mary put them right into the milk as soon as the calf began to suck them.

Then the little creature found that she was sucking up a great deal of milk! She still nuzzled around Aunt Mary's fingers, but she couldn't help taking in some of the milk in the pail, for her mouth was in it!

'That's a clever way of teaching her to drink milk,' said Lucy, delighted. 'Let me put *my* fingers in, Aunt Mary. I want to do it too.'

So Aunt Mary held the pail whilst Lucy dipped her fingers in, and let the calf suck them. Then slowly the little girl put them nearer to the milk, until once again the calf was drinking in the pail!

'She will soon learn,' said Aunt Mary. 'You can help me to feed the little thing three times a day, if you like, dear.'

So for the next week or two Lucy helped to feed the little calf. She loved her, and then one day she found that she was no longer afraid of cows!

'I can't be afraid of you when I love your little calf so much,' she told the big red and white cow. 'The little calf will grow up to be just like you, and she will give me presents like you do—milk and cream and butter and cheese. Thank you, cow. I'm sorry I ever said you were horrid. I like you now, big red cow, and one day I'll help to milk you!'

'Moo-ooo-ooo!' said the cow, pleased. 'Moo-ooo-oooo!'

Old Ugly the Water Grub

Once upon a time there was an ugly grub that lived in a little pond.

At first it was only small, but as time went on it grew. It had a long body, with many joints, and six legs on which it could crawl about in the mud.

The other creatures in the pond thought it was very ugly indeed. 'Look at it!' said the pretty little stickleback. 'I'd be ashamed of myself if I was as ugly as that!'

'I don't like its face,' said a water-snail with a nicely-curved shell. 'There's something wrong with its face.'

'Let's call it Ugly,' said a cheeky tadpole. 'Old Ugly! There goes Old Ugly! Hi, Old Ugly! What's wrong with your face?'

The grub did not like being called names. It could not help being ugly. Nor could it help its enormous appetite. It was always hungry.

The water-snail sometimes crawled near to where Old Ugly lay in the mud. 'Hallo, Old Ugly!' it would say. 'Would you like me for your dinner? Well, you can't have me, because I can always pop back into my shell-house if you come too near. What's the matter with your face, Old Ugly?'

Certainly the grub had a curious face. The water-snail used to watch him, and see it change.

Sometimes the grub would lie quietly in the water—and then perhaps a cheeky tadpole would swim too near him.

At once a strange thing happened to his face. The lower part of it seemed to fall away—and out would shoot a kind of claw that caught hold of the tadpole. The claw put the little creature to the grub's mouth—and that was the end of him.

Then the grub would fold up this curious claw, and put it by his face, so that it seemed part of it. The water-snail was very curious about it.

'Show me how it works,' he asked the grub. 'No—I'm not coming too near you—and I'm only going to put my head out just a little, in case you think of taking hold of it. Now—show me how that funny claw-thing works.'

The grub showed him. It was very clever the way he could fold it up below his face, so that it looked like part of it. It was on a hinge, and could be folded or unfolded just as he liked. 'It's a good idea,' said the water-snail. 'You are really rather a lazy creature, aren't you, Old Ugly—you like to lie about in the mud, and wait for your dinner to come to you. You don't like rushing about after it, like the water-beetle does. So that claw-thing is useful to you.'

'Very useful,' said the grub. 'I can just lie here and wait—and then shoot out my claw—like this!'

The water-snail shot his head in just in time. 'Don't play any tricks with *me*, Old Ugly,' he said. 'I tell you, I've got a hard shell. You could never eat me.'

Old Ugly the Water Grub

The other creatures in the pond were very careful not to go too near the grub. When they saw his face looking up out of the mud, they swam away quickly.

'That dreadful face!' said a gnat grub. 'It is horrid the way it seems to fall to pieces when that lower part, the claw, shoots out. It really gives me a fright. There he is—look! Hallo, Old Ugly!'

'Don't call me that,' said the grub. 'It hurts me. I can't help being what I am. It is not my fault that I am ugly.'

But nobody called him anything else. Nobody liked him. The snails teased him. The stickleback said that he would tear him to bits with his three spines if he went near his little nest of eggs. The tadpoles gathered round him at a safe distance and called him all the rude names they knew. And they knew a good many, for they were cheeky little things.

Even the frogs hated the grub. 'He snapped at my leg today,' said one. 'I didn't see him in the mud down there, and swam too near. Out shot that claw of his and gave my leg quite a nip.'

'Let's turn him out of the pond,' said the stickleback. 'We don't want him here. He is ugly and greedy and fierce. If we all get together, we can turn him out.'

So the stickleback, the frog, the two big black water-beetles, the tadpoles, the water-spider, the gnat grub, and the water-snails all swam or crawled to where Old Ugly was hiding in the mud, and called to him, 'We don't want you in the pond!'

'Go away from here or I will tear you with my spines!'

'Leave our pond, or we will chase you round and round it till you are tired out!'

Old Ugly's face fell apart, and he shot out his long claw in anger. 'How can I go away? There is nowhere for me to go to. I can't leave this pond. It is my home.'

'You must leave it by to-morrow or we will bite you,' said one of the water-beetles, the very fierce one.

'Yes, you must, or I shall rip you with my spines,' said the stickleback, and he went scarlet with rage.

Well, of course, there was nowhere that the ugly grub could go. He could not breathe out of the water. He could not catch his dinner except in the pond.

He was sad and frightened. Next day the other creatures came to him again. The stickleback rushed at him and nearly pricked him with his spines. The fierce water-beetle tried to bite his tail.

'Go away!' cried the water-creatures. 'Go away, Old Ugly.'

Old Ugly felt ill. There was the stem of a water-plant near by and he began to crawl up it.

'Leave me alone,' he said. 'I feel ill.'

The water-snail crawled after him. The stickleback tried to spear him with his spines. The grub went on up the stem, and at last came to the top of the water. He crawled right out of the water, and stayed there on the stem, still feeling strange.

'Has he gone?' cried the tadpoles. 'Has he gone?'

'He's out of the water,' said the water-snail. Then he stared hard at the grub. 'I don't think he feels very well,' he said. 'He looks a bit strange.'

The grub stood still on the stem, and waited. He didn't know what he was waiting for, but he knew that something was going to happen. He felt very strange.

114

Then, quite suddenly, the skin began to split across his head. The water-snail saw it and called down to the creatures below:

'His skin has split! He really is ill! Something strange is happening to Old Ugly.'

Something strange certainly *was* happening to the ugly grub. The skin split down his back too. Out from the top part came a head—a new head—a head with big brilliant eyes! The water-snail nearly fell from his leaf with astonishment.

'He's got a new head,' he said. 'And my goodness, he's got a new body too! His skin is splitting down his back. I can see his new body beneath.'

'Is it as ugly as his old one?' asked a tadpole.

'No—it's beautiful—it's wonderful!' said the snail, watching patiently. And, indeed, it *was* wonderful. As time went on, the grub was able to wriggle completely out of his old skin.

He was no longer an ugly grub. He was a most beautiful dragonfly! His body gleamed bright green and blue —and what a long body it was! He had four wings, big, shining ones that quivered in the sun. He had wonderful eyes.   He had six rather weak legs and a strong jaw.

'The ugly grub has changed into a dragonfly!' said the water-snail. 'Oh, what a strange thing to see! Dragonfly, what has happened?'

'I don't know!' said the dragonfly, glad to feel his wings drying in the sun. 'I don't know! I only know that for a long, long time I was an ugly grub in the pond— but that now I have wings, and I shall live in the air! Oh, what a wonderful time I shall have!'

When his wings were ready, the dragonfly darted high in the air on them, his blue and green body almost as bright as the kingfisher's feathers. He flew off, looking for insects to catch in his strong jaws. Snap—he caught a fly!

'What a beautiful creature!' said a little mouse in surprise, as the dragonfly whizzed past. 'Hi, Beauty, Beauty, Beautiful! Where are you going?'

'Are you talking to *me*?' said the dragonfly in surprise. 'I've always been called Old Ugly before!'

'You are lovely, lovely, *lovely*!' said the mouse. 'Stay and talk to me, do!'

But the dragonfly was off again, darting through the air on strong wings, as happy as a swallow.

'What a strange life I have had!' he hummed to himself. 'This is the nicest part. How happy I am, how happy I am!'

Maybe you will see him darting down the lane or over the pond. Look out for him, won't you, for he is one of the loveliest insects.

Adventures of the Sailor Doll

Once there was a sailor doll, and he lived in Janet's nursery. She was very fond of him, and he went everywhere with her. He was such a smart doll, with a blue velvet uniform and a nice sailor collar and round hat. He had a pink, smiling face, and was the most cheerful person you can imagine!

And then one day a dreadful thing happened to him. A puppy came into the garden where Janet was playing, and began to romp about. Janet was frightened and fled indoors. She left her sailor doll behind her on the grass! Oh, dear, what a pity!

The puppy saw the doll smiling up at him, and he picked it up in his teeth. He threw the doll into the air. The sailor stopped smiling, for he was frightened.

The doll came down on the grass. The puppy picked him up again and began to nibble him. He nibbled his hat and made a hole. He nibbled his sailor collar and tore it. He nibbled a shoe and got it off.

And then he did a really *dreadful* thing. He chewed one of the sailor's arms off! He bit it right off, and there it lay on the grass beside the poor scared doll.

Then there came a whistling, and the puppy's master came along. The puppy heard the whistling, ran to the gate, and darted out to his master. Off he went down the road, galloping along, leaving behind him the poor chewed sailor.

Well, Janet's mother very soon came out to clear up her little girl's toys, and she saw the sailor doll lying on the grass with his arm beside him. She was very sorry. She picked him up and looked at him.

'I'm afraid you're no more use,' she said. 'You'll have to go into the dust-bin, sailor. You are all chewed, and you have lost an arm.'

She put him on the seat and went on collecting the other toys. The sailor doll was so horrified at hearing he would have to go into the dust-bin that he lay and shivered. Then, seeing that Janet's mother was not looking, he quietly picked up his chewed arm, put it into his pocket, jumped down from the seat, and slipped away into the bushes. He wasn't going to be put into the dust-bin! Not he!

Janet's mother was surprised to find he had gone; but it was getting dark, so she went in with the other toys and didn't bother any more about the sailor. As soon as she had gone the sailor slipped out of the bushes and ran down the garden path. He went into the field at the end of the garden and walked over the grass.

He didn't know where he was going. He was just running away from the dust-bin. He went on and on, and soon the moon came up and lit everything clearly. Still he walked on. He met a hedgehog ambling along look-ing for beetles, and a mole with a long snout, and heard two mice quarrelling in the hedges. Still he went on— and at last he could go no further. He was really quite tired out. He had come to a little stream, and being a sailor doll he loved the sound of water.

'I think I'll settle down here for the night,' thought the sailor. 'I can go on in the morning. I think I am far enough away from that dust-bin now.'

So he crept under a dock leaf and lay down. Soon the moon went behind a great cloud, and it began to rain. A goblin crept under the dock leaf to shelter and, finding the sailor there, pushed him away. So the rain poured down on the poor sailor doll and soaked him through. He was so tired he didn't wake up till the morning—and then what a shock he had!

His sailor suit had shrunk in the rain and was now far too small for him. His hat had shrunk too, and looked very silly perched right on top of his head. His trouser legs were up to his knees, and his coat would no longer meet. He really looked dreadful.

He walked out into the sunshine, and how he sneezed, for he had caught a cold in the rain:

'A-tishoo! A-tishoo!'

'Hallo, hallo!' said a small voice, and the sailor doll saw a fairy peeping at him. 'What's the matter with you? You look a bit of a scarecrow! What are you?'

'I am supposed to be a sailor doll,' said the sailor humbly. 'I know I look dreadful now.'

'Well, you've got a bad cold,' said the fairy. 'Come into this rabbit-hole and I'll make a fire.'

The doll followed the fairy and to his enormous surprise he saw that down the rabbit-hole was a small door, neatly fitted into the side of the burrow. The fairy opened the door, and inside was a cosy room with a fire

119

laid. Soon it was crackling away cheerfully. He dried his clothes and felt more cheerful, especially when the fairy brought him some hot lemon and some ginger biscuits. Aha! This was good!

'You can stay here all day in the warmth, if you like,' said the fairy kindly.

'I am going to a boating party,' she said. 'It's being held on the stream. So you can sleep here all night, if you like. I shan't be back till dawn.'

'A boating party!' said the sailor doll, excited. 'Oh, can't I come?'

'No, it would be better for you to stay here in the warm and get rid of your cold,' said the fairy.

She put on a cape and ran out. The doll wished he knew what a boating party was like. He had never been to one. He opened the door and went into the rabbit-hole to see if he could hear any merry shouts and screams from the boating party. At first he heard laughter and shouts—and then he heard a great crying:

'Oh! Oh! You horrid frogs! Go away! You are spoiling our party!'

Then there came a sound of splashing and screaming. Whatever could be happening?

The doll ran out into the moonlight—and he saw a strange sight. The fairies had many little silver boats on the stream, and a great crowd of green frogs had popped up to sink the little boats.

One after another they were pulled under by the mischievous frogs. The fairies flew out of the boats as soon as they began to sink, but they were most unhappy because they had lost their pretty boats, and the party was spoilt.

The sailor doll ran to the bank in anger. 'How dare you do such a thing, frogs?' he cried. 'I will go and tell the ducks to come here and eat you!'

The frogs swam off in fright. But not a single boat was left!

'A-tishoo!' said the sailor doll. 'I am sorry I didn't come before!'

'Our party is spoilt!' wept the little fairies. 'We have no more boats—and oh, we were having such fun!'

A bright idea came into the sailor doll's head.

'I say,' he said, 'I know how to make boats out of paper. They float very well too. I used to watch Janet making them. If you can get me some paper, I could tell you how to make them.'

The fairies gave a shout of delight and ran off. Soon they came back with all sorts of pieces of paper, and they placed them in front of the doll.

'I wish I could make the boats for you,' he said, 'but, you see, I have only one arm, so can't. But I will tell you how to do it. Now—fold your paper in half to begin with.'

The fairies all did as he said, and soon there were dozens of dear little paper boats all ready to float on the river. Lovely!

The fairies launched them, and presently another boating party was going on. The frogs didn't dare to appear this time.

In the middle of the party a big ship with silver sails came floating down the stream.

'Look! Look! The Fairy King and Queen are sailing tonight, too!' shouted the fairies in glee.

'Let us float round them in our paper boats and give them a hearty cheer!'

121

So they did; and the King and Queen were *most* astonished to see such a fleet of boats appearing round their ship, full of cheering fairies.

'Go to the bank and anchor there,' the King commanded. So the ship was headed for the bank and very soon it was anchored there, and the fairies went on board.

'Who has taught you how to make these lovely boats?' asked the Queen, in surprise. 'I have never seen any like them before!'

'The sailor doll did,' said the little fairy who had helped the doll. She told the King all about the boating party spoilt by the frogs, and how the doll had taught them to make paper boats.

'Bring him here!' commanded the King. But the sailor doll was shy and didn't want to go before their majesties.

'I am all dirty and wet, and my suit is too small for me,' he said. 'Besides, I have lost an arm, and I am ashamed of having only one. Also, I have a bad cold, and I should not like to give it to the King or Queen. A-tishoo!'

So the fairy told the King what the doll had said, and the King nodded his head.

'See that the doll is given a new suit,' he said, 'and do what you can about his arm. Then send him to me at the palace. I want to speak to him about something very important.'

'You'll have to have a new suit altogether,' the fairy said. 'It wouldn't be any good patching up the one you have on. I can get you a new hat made too. The only thing that worries me is your arm. I don't know how I can get you one to match your own.'

'I wish I could make boats for all of you.'

'Oh, I've got my old one in my pocket,' said the sailor doll, and he pulled out his chewed arm.

'Oh, splendid!' said the fairy. 'Now I will go and fetch little Stitchaway the Pixie to measure you for a new suit. Sit by the fire and drink some more hot lemon. Your cold seems better already.'

She went out. The doll sat down by the fire. He was very happy. Things seemed to be turning out all right, after all.

Soon the fairy came back with a small pixie who had pin-cushions, scissors, and needle-books. With her she carried a great bunch of bluebells.

'Good-day, sailor,' she said. 'I shall have to make your suit of bluebells. I hope you won't mind, but that is the only blue I have at the moment. Now, stand up, and let me measure you.'

It didn't take long to measure the sailor. No sooner was this done than two more pixies appeared. One was a shoe-maker, and he soon fitted a pair of fine black boots on the sailor and took away his old ones. Then the other pixie, who was a hatter, and wore about twenty different hats piled on his head, tried them all on the sailor, and found a little round one that fitted him exactly. It had a blue feather in it, but the fairy said that it looked very nice, so the sailor left it in.

'Now where's your arm?' said the fairy. The doll took his arm from the shelf where he had put it whilst he was being measured. The fairy fitted it neatly into his shoulder, said a few magic words, and let go. The arm was as good as ever! The doll could use it just as well as he could use the other one. He was so delighted!

In two days' time the dressmaker pixie came back with the grandest blue sailor suit of bluebells that you can imagine! When the sailor dressed himself in it, he did feel smart. The fairy looked at him in admiration.

'You look like the captain of a ship,' she said. 'Now come along to the palace and we'll see what the King wants.'

Well, what do you think His Majesty wanted? The captain of his fairy fleet was going to leave the sea and live in a little cottage with his wife. The King wanted another captain—and that was why he had sent for the sailor doll.

'Will you be my new captain?' he asked him. 'You look so cheerful, always smiling—and the way you sent off those wicked frogs, and taught the fairies how to make new boats, was wonderful. I'd very much like you to be my new captain.'

'Oh, Your Majesty, it's too good to be true!' cried the doll, blushing all over his smiling face. 'I promise you I will do my very best.'

'Very well. You are my Captain, then!' said the King. 'Now come and have tea with the Queen and our children. They are all longing to know how to make paper boats.'

And now the sailor doll is very important indeed, and everyone in Fairyland salutes him when he goes by. You should see him commanding his ship too! You would never think he was once a poor chewed doll who was nearly put in a dust-bin!

The Enchanted Bone

There was once a greedy tabby cat called Whiskers. No one dared to leave anything on the table in case he jumped up and got it. If he found the cupboard door open, he would slip inside—and then there would be no chicken, no meat, no pie left on the shelves, you may be sure.

Now one day Whiskers went to visit his cousin in Pixieland. His cousin was a wonderfully clever cat, black with great green eyes and a tail as long as a monkey's. He belonged to a witch and helped her with her spells. He was always pleased to see Whiskers and gave him a saucer of cream.

One day he told Whiskers about a marvellous magic bone that the witch owned.

'Do you know, Whiskers,' said the black cat, 'that bone is so magic that if you put it on a plate and say:

> 'Bone, please multiply yourself,
> And give me meat to fill my shelf'—

it will at once make more and more and more bones, and you can get the most delicious soup all for nothing!'

The Enchanted Bone

Whiskers' eyes nearly fell out of his head with surprise. What a bone! If only he had one like that! He would always be able to have a fine meal then.

'Where does the witch keep that bone?' he asked.

'In the cupboard over there,' said the black cat, 'but it's always locked.'

Whiskers had a good look at the cupboard. Yes, it certainly was locked. There was no doubt about that.

But, do you know, the next time that Whiskers went to visit his cousin, that cupboard door was open! Yes, it really was! And what was more, both the witch and her black cat were away!

'Well, well, well!' said Whiskers in delight. 'Here's a chance for me. I'll borrow that bone this morning and make myself a fine collection of bones out of it, and then bring it back again before the witch and my cousin come back.'

He slipped into the cupboard. He jumped up on to the shelf. He saw the magic bone there, and taking it in his mouth he jumped down. Then out of the kitchen he went at top speed, the big enchanted bone in his mouth.

He ran home. He took the bone into the back garden and set it down on an old enamel plate, belonging to Spot the dog. And then Whiskers said the magic spell:

'Bone, please multiply yourself,
And give me meat to fill my shelf!'

The bone began to work. My goodness, you should have seen it! It was really marvellous. A big bone grew out of one end and fell on to the plate. A joint of meat

127

grew out of the other end and fell right off the plate. Whiskers stared in the greatest surprise and delight. What a feast he would have! Oh, what a feast!

The bone went on throwing out more bones and more joints. Soon the back garden smelt of meat, and Spot the dog woke up in surprise. He sat up. Meat! Bones! Where could they be? He raced over to Whiskers and stared at the meat and the bones in astonishment. Then he pounced on a bone.

'It's mine! It's mine! Drop it, Spot!' hissed Whiskers. But Spot wouldn't. He crunched up the bone and then started on a joint of meat.

The next-door dog sniffed the meat and came running in at the gate. The two dogs next door but one smelt it too and tore in, yelping happily. Whiskers didn't like strange dogs. He hissed and spat. But they took no notice of him and began to eat all the meat and bones.

That was too much for Whiskers. He wasn't going to have all his magic wasted like that. He caught up the enchanted bone and ran off with it. But it wouldn't stop growing bones and meat, and soon half the dogs in the town were after Whiskers in delight.

Whiskers was frightened almost out of his life. He took one look round at the dogs and fled on and on. He didn't dare to drop the magic bone, for he knew it would be eaten if he did and then what would the witch say?

He ran right round the town and back again. He came to his own house once more. The door was open. Whiskers ran inside and jumped up on to the table.

'Get down, Whiskers, get down!' shouted the cook, and she stared in astonishment—for into her kitchen poured dozens of dogs, black dogs, white dogs, brown

He caught up the enchanted bone and ran off with it.

dogs, spotted dogs, little ones and big ones, nice ones and nasty ones!

'Shoo! Shoo!' cried the cook. Whiskers mewed in fright and jumped up on to the top shelf of the dresser. The dogs jumped too—and crash, smash, crash, smash, down went cups and saucers, dishes and plates. The cook yelled in rage but more and more came in!

Then the cook saw that there was only one way of getting rid of them. She picked up the bones and meat that seemed everywhere—on the floor and the table and the dresser—and threw them out into the street as fast as she could. Out went all the dogs after them! Soon the kitchen was empty and the cook slammed the door. She glared at Whiskers.

'What do you mean by stealing all that meat and bringing it home?' she said.

Poor Whiskers got a dreadful scolding. He leapt out of the window, still with the magic bone in his mouth. He tore off with it to the witch's house—no dogs following this time because they were all busy in the street, gobbling up the meat and the bones that the cook had thrown out for them.

The witch was at home. So was the black cat. And how they glared at Whiskers when he came in with the stolen bone. The black cat flew at Whiskers and scratched him down the nose.

'Never come here again,' he mewed. 'You deserve to be well punished.'

'I have been punished,' mewed Whiskers. 'I shall never steal again—not even the hind leg of a kipper!'

He never did—and as for bones, he wouldn't go near them, no matter how nice they smelt! Poor old Whiskers!

Feefo Goes to Market

Once upon a time there was a gnome called Feefo who made a lot of money out of onion puddings. He grew specially big onions in his garden, and when they were ready he made them into such delicious puddings that you could smell them for miles.

Feefo had a wife and nine children, so although he made a lot of money he never grew rich, because there was always so much to buy for his children.

One day he sold sixteen onion puddings and made so much money that he really thought he would go and have a Big Spend. So he called his wife and asked her what he should spend his money on.

'You shall each have something,' he said, rattling his money. 'Tell me what you would like.'

'Buy me a beautiful new hat,' said his wife, beaming all over her face. 'I'd like that very much. And buy nine buckets and nine spades for the children to dig with. They are always asking for those.'

'Very well,' said Feefo. 'I will go to the town next market-day and buy all those things for you and the children. And for myself I will buy a red waistcoat. I have always wanted one.'

Mrs Feefo was so delighted to think she had such a generous husband that she popped in next-door to her neighbour, Mother Apple, and told her all about it.

'Feefo is buying me a new hat next market-day,' she said proudly. 'And he is getting the nine children a bucket and spade each. What do you think of that?'

Mother Apple thought a lot about it, but she didn't say much to Mrs Feefo. She kept it all for Father Apple when he came home that night.

'Why can't you be generous like Mr Feefo, the gnome?' she cried. 'He is getting his nine children a bucket and spade each and a new hat for his wife. You never buy *your* family anything like that!'

Mother Apple told Dame Tickles about it, and Dame Tickles wished that Mr Tickles was as generous as the gnome Feefo. She told him so when he came home, and he grew quite cross. She told Mrs Twiddle about it too, and Mrs Twiddle told her neighbour, Mother Bun, how generous the gnome Feefo was to his wife and children; and they all of them scolded their husbands because they didn't go to the market and buy hats and buckets and spades.

Now Father Apple, Mr. Tickles, Mr. Twiddle and Father Bun felt very cross with Feefo for being so generous.

'What does he want to go buying things like that for?' they said to one another. 'It only makes our wives and children think we are mean because we don't do the same. We ought to do something about it.'

Poor Apple, Twiddle, Tickles and Bun! Wherever they went they heard about the gnome Feefo going to market on Saturday to get a new hat and spades and buckets. And at last they put their heads together and thought of a plan.

'We will lie in wait for him at the bottom of Breezy Hill,' they said. 'We will jump out at him and take away all the things he has bought, and then he will not be able to go home and give presents to his wife and children.'

So on Saturday they set off to Breezy Hill, after seeing Feefo the gnome walking off to market, jingling his money in his pocket.

'It is hot,' said Father Bun. 'Let's go and sit on the top of the hill where there is a breeze. We shall easily see Feefo coming and can get down to the bottom long before he is at the top.'

So up the hill they went and sat down in a ring on the top. Twiddle ate a toffee, Bun chewed a grass, and the other two just sat and did nothing, feeling rather sleepy. Soon Twiddle pointed away in the distance, and said that he could see Feefo coming home from market.

Down the hill they went and hid in the bracken at the bottom, meaning to jump out at the gnome when he came walking by.

Feefo had a lot to carry. He had the hat and nine buckets and nine spades—and a fine red waist coat for himself. They were all very awkward to carry and when he reached the top of Breezy Hill he stopped to have a rest.

He sat down and mopped his head. Then he suddenly caught sight of a small yellow button lying not far off. He picked it up.

'Father Bun has been here,' he said to himself. 'He's been sitting down over there. Dear me, the grass is very

133

flattened just there. He must have had some others with him.'

He poked, about and found a toffee paper, which he looked at very closely.

'Now who eats these toffees?' he thought. Let me see—yes, Mr Twiddle does. He's been here too, and not so long ago, either. And here's a handkerchief left behind. It's got a name on it—Tickles. Ho, so he's been here too. That means that Apple was here as well, because they do everything together. Now why should Twiddle, Apple, Tickles and Bun all come up here on this hill today and sit here together?

He sat down and thought. Then he got up and looked on every side of the hill, shading his eyes with his hand.

'They're nowhere to be seen,' he said. 'That's funny. Are they hiding somewhere? And if they are hiding, why should they do such a funny thing?'

Then Feefo suddenly guessed that Twiddle, Tickles, Apple and Bun were keeping a look-out for him, and meant to jump on him and take away the things he had bought. And he sat down and grinned to himself. He would go down the hill all right but he didn't think they would jump on him. Ho, ho!

Feefo got some string out of his pocket and tied the spades in a row together. He slung them over his left shoulder. Then he strung the handles of the buckets together and slung these over his right shoulder. Then he put the red waist coat and the new hat on. How strange he looked!

'Now here we go!' he said to himself with a big grin on his cheeky face. He began to run down the hill, and as he ran he shouted at the top of his voice.

'Ho, ho, ho! Make way for Hanky-Panky, the Snorting Bing-Bong with his clinking, clanking, clonking Fire-eaters! Ho, ho, ho here I come, Hanky-Panky, snorting and snuffling, the great and dangerous Bing-Bong!'

As he ran and bounded in the air, all the nine buckets clanged together and all the spades crashed on one another, making a simply fearful din.

Goodness, what a fearful sight he looked, and what an awful noise he made! How the spades crashed and smashed together, how the buckets clanked and clinked, and as for the hat, it gave everyone a fright.

'Ho, ho, ho! Make way for Hanky-Panky, the Snorting Bing-Bong with his clinking, clanking, clonking Fire-eaters! Ho, ho, ho! Here I come, Hanky-Panky, snorting and snuffling, the great and dangerous BING-BONG!'

When Twiddle, Bun, Tickles and Apple heard this terrible noise and saw this awful creature tearing down the hill with a great hat on his head, banging and clanking, with long strings of things crashing behind him, they fell over one another with fright.

'Get out of his way, quick! Get out of his way!' they cried to one another, and they fell over each other's legs in their hurry. Poor Twiddle had fallen asleep whilst he was waiting, and he awoke to see the terrifying creature racing down the hill not far from him. He was so frightened that his legs bent under him when he tried to run, and he fell, bumping his nose on the ground.

Feefo the gnome was enjoying himself very much. On and on he ran, shouting and jumping high into the air, all the tin buckets and spades flying out behind him, making more noise than ever, trying not to laugh at the

135

sight of the four scrambling gnomes in front of him, struggling their hardest to get out of his way.

He passed them at a run, leaping his highest, whilst they dived into the bracken and hid, trembling and shaking. Then, when he had left them well behind him, Feefo sank down on the ground and began to laugh. The tears came into his eyes and ran down his long nose to the ground, where they made a big puddle.

How he laughed! He rolled on the ground and roared till his sides ached. Then he sat up and wiped his eyes.

'Dear, dear me,' he said. 'What a joke that was! I shall never laugh so much again. Ho, ho! Make way for Hanky-Panky, the Snorting Bing-Bong!'

He got to his feet, took the hat off his head and went peacefully home. He gave his wife and children their presents and they were delighted. Then he went to lean over his front gate, waiting for Twiddle, Bun, Tickles and Apple to come home.

At last they came, looking white and scared, turning round to look behind them every now and again.

'Hallo!' called Feefo. 'What's the matter?'

'Oh, Feefo, didn't you see the Snorting Bing-Bong with his clinking, clanking, clonking Fire-eaters?' cried Twiddle. 'He came tearing down Breezy Hill not so long ago.'

'Yes, it was Hanky-Panky, snorting and snuffling, the great and dangerous Bing-Bong,' said Bun, trembling. 'He trod on my toe when he passed and it has swelled up to twice its size.'

'He's a fearful person,' said Apple. 'Didn't you see him, Feefo? He's twice as big as you are, and wears an enormous hat.'

'Oh, yes, I know Bing-Bong,' said Feefo. 'He's a great friend of mine. I know him as well as I know myself, and I'm very fond of him. I know why he came, too.'

'Why?' asked Twiddle, in surprise.

'He came because he knew that there were enemies waiting for me round the corner,' said Feefo solemnly. 'He came to eat them up. Fancy that! No wonder you were frightened when you met him.'

Twiddle, Tickles, Bun and Apple looked very guilty, indeed. Could it really be that the Bing-Bong had known of their plan to jump on Feefo that afternoon? Ooh, what an escape they had had!

'Where is he now?' asked Apple fearfully.

'He's here,' said Feefo. 'Would you like to see him?'

'OOOOOOOOOOH!' shouted Twiddle, Bun, Apple and Tickles in a great fright, and they took to their heels and ran away as fast as ever they could.

Well, well! He hasn't a single enemy now, and I'm sure I don't wonder at it!

Fiddle-de-Dee the Foolish Brownie

Fiddle-de-dee was a young brownie. He lived with his mother in Pudding Cottage, and was very lazy indeed.

He simply wouldn't do a thing to help his mother.

'Now look here, Fiddle-de-dee,' she said one day. 'You really must help me. Your aunt and uncle are coming to tea, and I want some nice fresh muffins. You must go to the baker's and buy twelve.'

So Fiddle-de-dee set off. He bought twelve muffins at the baker's and then started off home. On the way back he felt tired, so he jumped into a bus. At the next stop so many people got in that some had to stand.

'May I sit on your knee?' another brownie asked Fiddle-de-dee.

'Certainly,' said Fiddle-de-dee—but he had the bag of muffins on his knee, and he wondered what to do with them. He slipped them underneath him, and then pulled the brownie down on to his knee. When the end of the ride came, the other brownie thanked him and they both got off the bus. The bag of muffins looked very squashed.

How cross Fiddle-de-dee's mother was when she saw them!

'You stupid, silly fellow!' she cried. 'You've been sitting on them!'

'Well, I had to put them somewhere,' said Fiddle-de-dee. 'If I hadn't sat on them the other brownie would have, for he sat on my knee. And as he was a lot heavier than I am, I thought it would be better if I sat on them!'

'You didn't think that you were both sitting on them, then?' asked his mother. 'Now, listen, Fiddle-de-dee— the next time I send you out you must think what you're doing. You should have asked the baker to lend you a tray, and then you should have walked home with the muffins on your head like the muffin man.'

'I see,' said Fiddle-de-dee, determined to do better next time.

Now two days later his mother thought it would be nice to have some ice-cream, for the day was hot. So she gave Fiddle-de-dee a coin and told him to fetch some from the ice-cream shop. He set off, and bought a nice lot. It was in a cardboard box.

He had just left the shop when he remembered how he had been scolded about the muffins.

'Mother said I ought to have brought them home on my head,' he said. 'Well, I forgot to borrow a tray this time, but I'm sure I can balance this box on my head all right.'

So he popped the box of ice-cream on his head, and walked home with it. But the sun was tremendously hot that day and beat down on Fiddle-de-dee all the way home. The ice-cream soon melted and began to run out of the corners of the box. It ran down Fiddle-de-dee's hair and trickled down his neck.

'Ooh!' said Fiddle-de-dee in surprise. 'I do feel nice and cold. It isn't such a hot day after all. I'm not nearly so hot now.'

The ice-cream went on trickling down his head and neck all the way home. When his mother saw him she gave a cry of dismay.

'Fiddle-de-dee!' she cried. 'Whatever are you doing with the ice-cream, carrying it on your head like that in the hot sun! Oh, how foolish you are! It is all melted now, and you are in a terrible mess! You should have wrapped a damp cloth round the box, and covered it with your coat to keep it cool.'

'Oh,' said Fiddle-de-dee. 'Well, how was I to know that? I'll do better next time.'

The next day his mother heard that a fine goose was for sale, and she was determined to buy it and keep it for Christmas-time.

'I'll fatten it up,' she said, 'and when Christmas comes it will make us a good Christmas dinner.'

So she sent Fiddle-de-dee to get it. He bought it from the farmer, and set off with the goose. But he hadn't gone very far before he remembered how his mother had scolded him about the ice-cream.

'She said I ought to have wrapped it in a damp cloth and carried it home under my coat,' he said. 'Well, I must try to take the goose home as she said.'

Hanging on a near-by clothes-line was a tablecloth belonging to Mother Wimple. Fiddle-de-dee took it down and soaked it in a pond. Then he wrapped the struggling, angry goose in it, and tried to put it under his coat. But the bird was big and strong, and it was all Fiddle-de-dee could do to hold it.

Fiddle-de-Dee the Foolish Brownie

By the time he reached home his coat and shirt were torn by the goose in its struggles to escape. The tablecloth was in rags, and Fiddle-de-dee was all hot and bothered.

'Oh my, oh my!' groaned his mother, when she saw him. 'What *have* you been doing with Mother Wimple's lovely new tablecloth? And just look at your clothes, Fiddle-de-dee! They're only fit for the dustbin now! And the poor goose is half dead with fright!'

'I tried to do as you said,' said Fiddle-de-dee, 'but the goose didn't like being wrapped up in a damp cloth, Mother.'

'You stupid, foolish boy,' said his mother. 'Can't a goose walk? You should have tied a string round its neck and let it follow behind you!'

'I see,' said Fiddle-de-dee, and made up his mind to do better next time.

A week later his mother wanted him to fetch the joint of meat from the butcher's, so he set off. He took the leg of mutton from the man, and turned to go home. Then he remembered how angry his mother had been with him last time he had gone on an errand for her, and he tried to think how he should take the meat home.

'Mother said last time I ought to have tied a string to the goose's neck and let it follow behind me!' he thought. 'Well, this mutton's got a leg, so I'll tie some string to it.'

He found a piece of string in his pocket and carefully tied it to the leg of mutton. Then he threw it behind him, and set off home, dragging the meat after him.

He hadn't gone far when half the dogs and cats in the neighbourhood smelt the meat and came running after it. Fiddle-de-dee turned round and saw them all.

He became frightened and started to run. All the dogs and cats ran too!

He tore home, the meat bumping up and down behind him. He raced in through the kitchen door—and all the cats and dogs came too, snarling, growling and fighting over the leg of mutton!

'Oh, good gracious, oh, my goodness!' cried his mother. 'Whatever will you do next? What made you bring these creatures home with you? Oh dear, oh dear, look at that meat! You surely haven't dragged it home on a piece of string!'

'Well, that's what you told me to do with the goose, Mother,' said Fiddle-de-dee.

'Yes, but a leg of mutton isn't a goose!' cried his mother. Then she shooed the dogs and cats away.

'Shoo, shoo, shoo!' she shouted. 'Shoo, you cats, shoo, you dogs!'

When all the animals had gone away she turned to scold Fiddle-de-dee—but he wasn't there. He had gone to put himself to bed! He thought that would be the best place for him that day, and he was quite right!

Goblin's Pie

There was once a goblin called Roundabout who was greedy. The thing he liked best of all was a pie. It didn't matter what *kind* of a pie—meat-pie, chicken-pie, veal-and-ham pie, apple-pie, plum-pie, onion-pie—he liked them all.

His friends wished he wouldn't be so greedy. They really were afraid he would burst out of his clothes one day. But Roundabout took no notice of his friends. He just went on eating and eating.

He would walk miles for a pie. Yes, really! When he heard that Dame Strawberry had baked three fine strawberry-pies one day he set out to get one. Dame Strawberry lived on Tree-Top Hill miles away, but that didn't matter. Round-about walked and walked until he got there, and he arrived the day after tomorrow.

Well, of course, all the pies were eaten by then, except for a tiny piece. But Roundabout ate that and said it was worth walking all those miles for!

Now one day Pinny, one of his friends, thought he would have a joke with Roundabout. He was walking out with him in the woods, and suddenly Pinny saw a big bird, a black and white magpie, sitting on a tree nearby.

'Roundabout!' said Pinny solemnly, stopping quite still. 'Shall I tell you something?'

'Yes, do,' said Roundabout, 'especially if it's about something to eat. I feel hungry.'

'That's nothing new,' said Pinny. 'Well, now listen—there's a pie up in that tree. Look!'

Pinny pointed to the tree in which the magpie sat. Round-about licked his lips and looked up at the tree. He thought that Pinny meant a real pie.

'Is it a meat-pie?' he asked.

'It's a bird-pie,' said Pinny, laughing to himself.

'I can't see it,' said Roundabout.

'Well, go and look for it,' said Pinny.

Roundabout at once went to the tree and began to climb it. He found it very difficult, but he wouldn't give up if there was a pie anywhere about—no, not he! Up he went, panting and puffing, looking for that pie.

How he looked! He peered down into the trunk. He put his hand into every hole. He parted the leaves and looked carefully where they grew the thickest. But he couldn't find any pie.

He climbed higher up and looked there. The big magpie looked at him, puzzled. What was this goblin doing? Was he looking for her nest?

She began to chatter angrily at him. He looked at her in surprise.

'What's the matter?' he asked. 'Are you looking for that pie too?'

'Pie? What pie?' asked the big bird. 'There isn't any pie here, I can tell you! This tree is mine.'

'Nonsense!' said Roundabout. 'You can't take trees for yourself like that. Tell me where that pie is.'

'It's a bird-pie,' said Roundabout.

'I don't know *where* it is,' said the magpie crossly. I'm sure there isn't one in my tree. I wish you'd go away. What do you want with a pie, anyway?'

'I want to eat it,' said Roundabout. 'I'm very hungry.'

'What's the pie like?' asked the magpie, thinking that perhaps she might have a peck at it too.

'It's a bird-pie,' said Roundabout, 'and it's in this tree, I know.'

No sooner had he said that than the bird remembered that her name was magpie. She at once thought that the goblin was looking for her or for her little ones. She was very angry indeed, and she flew at the surprised goblin.

'So you came to eat *me*, did you?' she cried in a rage. 'Take that! Peck-peck-peck!'

Roundabout nearly fell off the branch in surprise. He held on tightly, and tried to stop the magpie from pecking him, but she was far too cross to stop.

'Peck-peck-peck!' She pecked off his round hat and threw it to the ground. She pecked off his coat and made two big holes in it. She pecked a big piece out of his trousers and pulled off both his shoes.

'Stop, stop!' cried Roundabout in a panic. 'I'll climb down at once if you'll stop pecking me. I don't care about any pie. I'll get down and never come here again.'

The magpie gave him one more peck for luck, and then let Roundabout get down. He was in such a hurry that he fell down part of the way, and bounced, like a rubber ball on the grass.

'Goodness!' he cried. 'That's the last time I go after pies.'

He found his shoes and his hat. He picked up his coat and looked at the two big holes. He stuffed a large green leaf into his trousers to hide the hole there, and then he looked about for Pinny, his friend. But Pinny had gone back to the village to tell the folk what a joke he had played on Roundabout, sending him up a tree to look for a pie to eat—when all the time there wasn't a pie at all, but only a magpie.

All the little folk came running out of the village to see the fun—and they met poor Roundabout limping back, looking very sorry for himself.

'Hallo!' he said, when he saw Pinny. 'I didn't find that pie you told me about—and a very nasty bird nearly pecked me to pieces!'

'Poor Roundabout!' said Pinny. 'That bird was the pie—it was a magpie. I didn't think it would set about you like that.'

'Good gracious, was that the pie?' asked Roundabout, surprised. 'Well, no wonder it got angry when I said I wanted to eat it! That's taught me a lesson. I'll never eat a pie again!'

Roundabout kept his word for two whole days, and then, I'm sorry to say, someone sent him an apple-pie—and he ate it all up before you could say 'Jack Robinson'!

But you've only got to mention Magpie to make him shiver all over!

Good Old Jumbo!

Outside the nursery window lived three small pixies called Binks, Jinks and Dimple. The toys knew them very well indeed, for the pixies came into the nursery every night when it was dark, and played with them.

Binks and Jinks were big strong pixies, but Dimple was small and sweet. She was their sister, and they loved her very much. All the toys were good to her and she rode in the wooden train, in the toy motor car and in the clockwork train as many times as she liked.

She liked all the toys except big Jumbo, the grey elephant. He had once trodden on her toe by accident, and she was frightened of him. He was so big and clumsy. Jumbo was sad about it, because he liked Dimple very much, and was always longing to give her a ride on his back. But she never would ride on him.

The toys belonged to two children, Amy and Michael. But lately the children hadn't bothered at all about their toys, because Uncle Jim had given them something they liked much better—two pairs of roller skates! You should have seen how Amy and Michael tore round and round the garden paths on their skates! Goodness, they went like lightning!

The toys were jealous of the roller skates. The children kept them in the toy cupboard but every night the toys pushed them out. They didn't like them.

'They are nasty things,' said the old teddy bear. 'I don't know why the children like them better than they like us. Get out of the toy cupboard, you ugly things! You don't belong here!'

Then bump-bump! Out would tumble the four skates on to the floor. They weren't alive, so they didn't mind one way or another. But the children were always puzzled to know how it was their skates fell out of the toy cupboard so often!

The toys played by themselves each night, and were very glad when the three pixies came to join them.

'It's nice to have *somebody* to play with,' said the teddy bear. 'The children hardly ever take any notice of us now!'

One night Binks and Jinks came in at the window in a great hurry, looking as scared as could be.

'Toys, toys! What shall we do? Six red goblins came tonight and stole away Dimple, our little pixie sister! Oh whatever shall we do?'

The toys turned pale with fright. The red goblins were nasty creatures, with claws instead of nails and they could scratch just like cats.

'We could never catch up with the goblins!' said the old teddy bear. 'They go so fast!'

'Well, you can't ask *me* to go after them,' said the clock-work train, in a hurry. 'I can only run on my rails.'

'And my key is lost,' said the clockwork motor car. '*I* can't go!'

'Nobody wants to go!' wailed the two pixies sorrowfully. 'Poor Dimple! She'll never come back again.'

Then the big elephant, Jumbo, spoke in his big deep voice.

'*I* will go and chase those goblins!' he said. '*I'm* not afraid!'

'But dear old Jumbo, you're so slow and clumsy!' cried all the toys together.

'Ah, but I've got a splendid idea!' said Jumbo. 'I want you to strap those roller skates on to my big feet. Then I shall go like the wind, roller-skating down all the paths to Goblin-Land!'

Well, what an idea! Did you ever hear anything like it! I never did. Anyway, you should have seen how the toys and the two pixies clapped their hands when they heard what Jumbo said. They thought it was the best idea they had ever heard.

'Quick! Get the roller skates!' cried Binks and Jinks. Where are they?'

Old Teddy got one, teddy bear found another, and the two biggest dolls brought the last two. Then they strapped them on to Jumbo's big, clumsy feet. He *did* look funny!

'I'm just going to have a skate round the nursery to see if I can do it properly,' said Jumbo, shaking with excitement. Crash-crash-crash went his feet, as he tried his hardest to skate with all four at once. Dear me, you should have seen him!

All the toys got out of his way in a great hurry, for his four feet shot out all over the place, and he didn't know at all where he was going. He knocked the old teddy down flat on his nose and ran over the teddy bear's big toe. Goodness, it was a sight to see!

'Steady on, Jumbo! called Binks, jumping up on to a chair for safety. 'Oh, good gracious!'

Jumbo bounced into the chair and sent it flying! Down fell poor Binks with a crash. Up he got and climbed up on to the window-sill, feeling certain that Jumbo couldn't knock that down!

After a little while Jumbo began to skate much better. His legs went properly and he found that he could skate right round the nursery and back again without falling over once. He did feel proud.

'Now I'm ready to go after Dimple and the goblins,' he said to the pixies. 'Jump up on my back and tell me the right way to go.'

Binks and Jinks jumped up on to his broad back, and hung on tightly. Crash-crash-crash went the roller skates as Jumbo skated out of the room and down the passage to the garden. What a noise he made! It's a wonder nobody heard him!

The moon was shining brightly. Down the garden path went Jumbo, skating splendidly. If one of his feet slipped he still had three others to help him, so he didn't fall over at all.

He *did* go at a rate! Out into the lane he skated and over the hill. Then down a large rabbit-hole to Goblin-Land.

The streets of Goblin-Land are very straight and smooth, so Jumbo found he could go at top speed there! Crash-crash-crash went his skates and he tore along faster than any motor car could possibly go. Binks and

Jinks soon lost their hats, for the wind streamed past them and snatched away their hats with greedy fingers.

'There they are, there they are!' suddenly shouted Binks, so loudly that he frightened Jinks and nearly made him fall off Jumbo's back. Jumbo looked in front of him and saw a crowd of little red goblins riding yellow rocking-horses. One of them held Dimple tightly in his arms, whilst he shouted to his rocking-horse to rock faster and faster through Goblin-Land.

Jumbo made a sound like a trumpet and skated on faster than ever. The goblins heard the crash of his roller skates and looked back. When they saw Jumbo behind them on skates, carrying Binks and Jinks on his back, they could hardly believe their eyes. They shouted to the rocking-horses.

'Go on! Go on! Faster still! Hurry, hurry, hurry!'

The rocking-horses rocked away till it seemed as if they must tumble on their noses or tails. They went very fast indeed. But Jumbo went even faster. How he skated! You could hardly see his legs moving, they went so quickly.

'They're taking Dimple to the Deep Green Cave!' suddenly cried Binks. 'Oh dear, catch them before they get there, Jumbo, or we shall never see our dear little sister again!'

Sure enough, the goblins were going to the Deep Green Cave. Jumbo saw the mountain in which it was, and he skated even faster to get there before the goblins did—and he got there at exactly the same minute. Then you should have seen him fighting those goblins. Binks and Jinks joined in too and fought the goblins bravely.

Good Old Jumbo!

'Let's go and get the green goblins to help us!' suddenly shouted a red goblin to his friends. So they all rushed into the Deep Green Cave to get help, and left Dimple, Binks and Jinks with Jumbo outside.

'On my back, quick, all of you!' shouted Jumbo, in his trumpeting voice. Binks and Jinks jumped up, and helped Dimple. She had quite forgotten that she had said she never, never would ride on Jumbo, but got up as quickly as she could.

Then back went Jumbo, skating as fast as his four legs would take him. Long before the green and the red goblins came running out of their cave Jumbo was out of sight, crash-crash-crashing along on his four roller skates!

'On my back, quick, all of you!' shouted Jumbo.

153

It didn't take him long to get back to the nursery, very much out of breath, but simply delighted with himself. He had got dear little Dimple on his back at last! The toys gave him a great welcome, and cheered him with all their might. His trunk blushed quite red with pride.

The toys unstrapped the skates from his tired feet and put them away again. Then they heard the first cock crowing to say that day was coming, so they hurriedly said good-bye to the pixies and climbed back into the toy cupboard to go to sleep.

Binks and Jinks patted Jumbo before they went, but Dimple flung her arms round his trunk and kissed him lovingly.

'You're a dear, brave Jumbo,' she said, 'and I'm sorry I ever said you were clumsy. I'll come and ride on you every single night if you'll let me!'

Then off she went, and left Jumbo standing by himself, very happy indeed.

Gooseberry Whiskers

There was once a rascally gnome who sold fine paint-brushes to the fairies. No brushes were half as good as his, for the hairs in them were so fine and strong. 'Where do you get them from?' asked the elves one day. But the gnome wouldn't tell them.

'It's a secret,' he said. 'Perhaps I make them out of moonbeams drawn out long and thin, and snipped off in short pieces!'

'You don't!' cried the elves. 'Oh *do* tell us your secret!'

But he never would—and the reason was that he was afraid to. He got the hairs from sleeping caterpillars, and such a thing was not allowed in Fairyland, as you may guess. Many caterpillars were covered with soft fine hairs, and by pulling a few from this one and a few from that, the little gnome soon had enough for a new brush.

One spring-cleaning time there was a great demand for his brushes. All through May the elves came to buy from him and the gnome could hardly find enough caterpillars to pull hairs from!

He began to pull more than a few hairs from each. Once he took quite a handful, and the caterpillar woke up with a squeak.

Another furry caterpillar woke up one morning to find that he was quite bald. He hadn't a single hair left and he shivered with cold.

When the Queen passed by she stopped in surprise.

'But who could have taken your hairs away?' she asked the caterpillar. 'No one would do such a naughty thing.'

'Please, Your Majesty, someone must have done it last night,' said the caterpillar.

'And half *my* coat is gone too!' said another.

'And about thirty of my finest hairs have disappeared as well!' cried a third.

'This must be looked into,' said the Queen, sternly.

She called to her guards and spoke to them. 'Twelve of you must remain here to look after these caterpillars,' she commanded. 'You can hide under the hedge, and watch for the thief. Catch him and punish him well.'

The caterpillars crawled to their leaves. Now at last they would be safe! The twelve guards looked about for good hiding-places, and then played a game of snap until night-time, for they felt sure there would be no sign of the thief until darkness fell. The caterpillars were so interested in the game that they called 'Snap!' when they shouldn't, and made the guards quite cross.

'Don't interfere,' said the captain. 'We are playing, not you. You eat your juicy leaves, and don't disturb us or we will leave you to the robber!'

When night came the soldiers squeezed themselves into their hiding-places and kept watch. The night was dark, and it was difficult for them to see an inch in front of their noses. Just the night for a robber to come!

*Once he took quite a handful, and the caterpillar woke
with a squeak.*

Time went on. No thief. Ten o'clock came, eleven o'clock. Still no thief. The guards began to yawn. Surely the robber would not come now.

But at that very moment the little gnome was out on his rounds, looking for furry caterpillars. He was hunting under the leaves, down the stalks, on the ground, and everywhere. He didn't know that anyone was lying in wait for him.

He was very silent. His feet made no sound as he crept along, and he didn't even rustle a leaf.

'Where are all the caterpillars tonight?' he thought. I can't seem to find any!'

From bush to bush he went, feeling along the leaves, and at last he really did find a large furry caterpillar, peacefully sleeping.

'Good!' thought the gnome. 'This one has a fine crop of hairs! I can make a fine brush from them.'

He grabbed a big handful from the back of the sleeping caterpillar, and pulled hard. The caterpillar woke up with a loud squeak. 'Eee, eee, eee!' it cried.

At once all the guards sprang up and shouted loudly. 'The robber, the robber!'

The gnome fled away in terror, holding all the hairs in his hand. The guards ran after him, and went crashing through the woods into the palace gardens. Up and down the paths they went, searching for the thief. Where was he? Where had he gone?

The little gnome had found a prickly hiding-place under a big gooseberry bush. He crouched there in fright, wondering what would happen to him if he was found. In his hand he still held the caterpillar hairs. Whatever could he do with them?

'The guards mustn't find them in my hand,' he thought. 'And I daren't throw them away, for they are sure to be found. What *can* I do?'

He put out his hand and felt about. He touched two or three big fat gooseberries—and then an idea came to him. He would stick the hairs on them, for surely no one would think of looking on the fruit for caterpillar hairs!

In a moment he was sticking the hairs on the green smooth surface of the gooseberries. He made them all hairy and whiskery, and just as he had finished, somebody came down the path near-by and flashed a lantern on to him.

'Here's someone!' they cried. 'Here's the thief! Quick, come and get him!'

The gnome was searched. No hairs were found on him, but in his pocket were two brushes that he had forgotten about and they were made of caterpillar hairs!

'Turn him out of Fairyland for ever!'

So the gnome was taken to the gates of Fairyland. They were shut behind him, and out he went, weeping bitterly.

No one has heard of him since—but from that day to this gooseberries have always grown whiskers. If you don't believe me, go and look for yourself!

Little Walking House

If it hadn't been for Puppy-Dog Pincher the adventure would never have happened. Jill and Norman were taking him for a walk in Cuckoo Wood. He tore here, there and everywhere, barking and jumping for all he was worth.

The children laughed at him, especially when he tumbled head over heels and rolled over and over on the grass. He was such a roly-poly puppy, and they loved him very much.

Then something happened. Pincher dived under a bramble bush, and came out with something in his mouth. It was a string of small sausages!

'Now wherever could he have got those from?' said Jill, in surprise. She soon knew, for out from under the bush ran a little fellow dressed in red and yellow, with a pointed cap on his head. He wasn't much taller than the puppy, but he had a very big voice.

'You bad dog!' he shouted. 'You've stolen the sausages I bought for dinner! Bring them back at once or I'll turn you into a mouse!'

Pincher took no notice. He galloped about with the sausages, enjoying himself very much. Then he sat down to eat them! That was too much for the small man. He rushed at Pincher and tapped him on the nose with a tiny silver stick. At the same time he shouted out a string of strange words, so strange that Jill and Norman felt quite frightened. They knew they were magic words, although they had never heard any before.

And then, before their eyes Pincher began to grow small! He grew smaller and smaller and smaller and smaller, and at last he was as tiny as a mouse. In fact, he *was* a mouse, though he didn't know it! He couldn't think what had happened to him. He scampered up to Jill and Norman, barking in a funny little mouse-like squeak.

The children were dreadfully upset. They picked up the tiny mouse and stroked him. Then they looked for the little man to ask him if he would please change Pincher back to a dog again.

But he had gone. Not a sign of him or his sausages was to be seen. Norman crawled under the bramble bush, but there was nothing there but dead leaves.

'Oh, Jill, whatever shall we do?' he said. 'We can't take Pincher home like this. Nobody would believe he was Pincher, and he might easily be caught by a cat.'

Jill began to cry. She did so love Pincher, and it was dreadful to think he was only a mouse now, not a jolly, romping puppy-dog.

'That must have been a gnome or a brownie,' she said, wiping her eyes. 'Well, Norman, I'm not going home with Pincher like that. Let's see if we meet any more little folk. If there's one here, there must be others. We'll ask them for help if we meet them.'

So they went on. Norman carried Pincher in his pocket, for there was plenty of room there for the little dog, now that he was only a mouse.

After they had gone a good way they saw the funniest little house. It had two legs underneath it, and it stood with its back to the children. Norman caught hold of Jill's arm and pointed to it in amazement. They had never seen a house with legs before.

'Oh!' cried Jill, stopping in surprise. 'It's got legs!'

The house gave a jump when it heard Jill's voice, and then, oh goodness me, it ran off! Yes, it really did! You should have seen its little legs twinkling as it scurried away between the trees. The children were too astonished to run after the house. They stood and stared.

'This is a funny part of Cuckoo Wood,' said Norman. 'Jill! Look! There are some more of those houses with legs!'

Jill looked. Sure enough, in a little clearing stood about six more of the houses. Each of them had a pair of legs underneath, and shoes on their big feet. They stood about, sometimes moving a step or two, and even stood on one leg now and again, which made the house they belonged to look very lop-sided.

Jill and Norman walked towards the funny houses— but as soon as they were seen, those houses took to their heels and ran off as fast as they could! The children ran after them, but they couldn't run fast enough.

They were just going to give up when they saw one of the houses stop. It went on again, but it limped badly.

'We could catch that one!' said Jill. 'Come on, Norman!'

They ran on and in a few minutes they had caught up with the limping house. Just as they got near it the door opened and a pixie looked out. She was very lovely, for her curly golden hair was as fine as spider's thread, and her wings shone like dragonfly wings.

'What's the matter, little house?' they heard her say. 'Why are you limping?'

Then she saw the children and she stared at them in surprise.

'Oh, so that's why the houses ran off!' she said. 'They saw you coming! Could you help me, please, children? I think my house has a stone in one of its shoes, and I'm not strong enough to get it out all by myself.'

Jill and Norman were ready to help. Norman held up one side of the house whilst the house put up one of its feet to have its big shoe off. The pixie and Jill found a big stone in the shoe, and after they had shaken it out they put on the shoe again. The little house made a creaking noise that sounded just like 'Thank you!'

'What a funny house you've got!' said Jill to the pixie.

'What's funny about it?' asked the pixie in surprise, shaking back her long curly hair. 'It's just the same as all my friends' houses.'

'But it's got legs!' said Norman. 'Where we come from, houses don't have legs at all. They just stand square on the ground and never move at all, once they are built.'

'They sound silly sort of houses,' said the pixie. 'Suppose an enemy came? Why, your house couldn't run away! Mine's a much better house than yours.'

'Oh, much better,' agreed Jill. 'I wish I lived in a house like this. It would be lovely. You'd go to sleep at night and wake up in a different place in the morning, because the house might wander miles away.'

'Pixie, I wonder if you could help us!' suddenly said Norman. He took the little mouse out of his pocket. 'Look! This was our puppy-dog not long ago and a nasty little man changed him into a mouse. Could you change him back into a dog again?'

'Oh no,' said the pixie. 'You want very strong magic for that. I only know one person who's got the right magic for your mouse, and that's High-Hat the Giant.'

'Where does he live?' asked Jill eagerly.

'Miles away from here,' said the pixie 'You have to go to the Rainbow's End, and then fly up to Cloud-Castle just half-way up the rainbow.'

'Goodness, we couldn't possibly go there,' said Jill. 'We haven't wings like you, Pixie.'

'Well, Dumpy the gnome lives near the Rainbow's End,' said the pixie. 'He keeps pigs that fly, you know, so he might lend you two of them. But I don't know if High-Hat the Giant will help you, even if you go to him. He's a funny-tempered fellow, and if he's in a bad mood he won't do anything for anybody.'

'Well, we might try,' said Norman. 'Which is the way to the Rainbow's End?'

'It depends where there's a rainbow today,' said the pixie. 'I know! I'll get my house to take you there. It always knows the way to anywhere. Come inside and we'll start. You helped me to get the stone out of my house's shoe, and I'd like to help you in return.'

The children went inside the house, feeling most excited. Norman had Pincher the mouse safely in his pocket. Pincher kept barking in his squeaky voice, for he couldn't understand how it was that Jill and Norman

'What a funny house you've got!' said Jill to the pixie.

had grown so big! He didn't know that it was himself that had grown small.

The pixie shut the door, and told the children to sit down. It was a funny house inside, more like a carriage than a house, for a bench ran all round the wall. A table stood in the middle of the room and on it were some dishes and cups. In a corner a kettle boiled on a stove, and a big grandfather clock ticked in another corner.

The clock had two feet underneath it, like the house, and it gave the children quite a fright when it suddenly walked out from its corner, had a look at them and then walked back.

'Don't take any notice of it,' said the pixie. 'It hasn't any manners, that old clock. Would you like a cup of cocoa and some daffodil biscuits?'

'Oooh yes, please,' said both the children at once, wondering whatever daffodil biscuits were. The pixie made a big jug of cocoa and put some funny yellow biscuits on a plate, the shape of a daffodil trumpet. They tasted delicious, and as for the cocoa, it was lovely—not a bit like ordinary cocoa, but more like chocolate and lemonade mixed together. The children did enjoy their funny meal.

Before the pixie made the cocoa she spoke to her house. 'Take us to the Rainbow's End,' she said. 'And be as quick as you can.'

To the children's great delight the house began to run. They felt as if they were on the sea, or on the elephant's back at the Zoo, for the house rocked from side to side as it scampered along. Jill looked out of the window. They were soon out of the wood, and came to a town.

'Norman, look! There are hundreds of fairy folk here!' cried Jill, in excitement. So there were—crowds of them, going about shopping, talking and wheeling funny prams with baby fairies inside. The grandfather clock walked out of its corner to the window too, and trod on Jill's toe. It certainly had no manners that clock.

They passed right through the town and went up a hill where little blue sheep were grazing. Looking after them was a little girl exactly like Bopeep. The pixie said yes, it really was Bopeep. That was where she lived. It was a most exciting journey, and the children were very sorry when they saw a great rainbow in the distance. They knew they were coming to the end of their journey in the walking house.

The little house stopped when it came to one end of the rainbow. The children stepped outside. There was the rainbow, glittering marvellously. It was very, very wide, far wider than a road and the colours were almost too bright to look at.

'Now High-Hat the Giant lives halfway up,' said the pixie, pointing. 'Come along, I'll take you to Dumpy the gnome, and see if he has a couple of pigs to spare you.'

She took them to a squat little house not far from the rainbow. Outside was a big yard and in it were a crowd of very clean pigs, bright pink and shining. Each of them had pink wings on his back, so they looked very strange to Jill and Norman.

'Hi, Dumpy, are you at home?' cried the pixie. The door of the house flew open and a fat gnome with twinkling eyes peeped out.

'Yes, I'm at home,' he said. 'What can I do for you?'

167

'These children want to fly to High-Hat's,' said the pixie. 'But they haven't wings. Could you lend them two of your pigs?'

'Yes, if they'll promise to be kind to them,' said Dumpy. 'The last time I lent out my pigs someone scolded them and all the curl came out of their tails.'

'Oh, these children helped me to take a stone out of my house's shoe,' said the pixie, 'so I know they're kind. You can trust them. Which pigs can they have, Dumpy?'

'This one and that one,' said the little gnome, and he drove two plump pigs towards the children. 'Catch hold of their tails, children, and jump on. Hold on to their collars, and, whatever you do, speak kindly to them or the curl will come out of their tails.'

Jill and Norman caught hold of the curly tails of the two pigs and jumped on. The pigs' backs were rather slippery, but they managed to stay on. Suddenly the little animals rose into the air, flapped their pink wings and flew up the shining rainbow. It was such a funny feeling. The pigs talked to one another in little squeals, and the children were careful to pat them kindly in case the curl came out of their tails.

In ten minutes they came to a towering castle, set right in the middle of the rainbow. It was wreathed in clouds at the top, and was made of a strange black stone that reflected all the rainbow colours, in a very lovely manner. It didn't seem a real castle, but it *felt* real enough when the children touched it. They jumped off the pigs' backs and patted them gratefully.

'Stay here, little pigs, till we come out again,' said Norman. Then he and Jill climbed up the long flight of shining black steps to the door of the castle. There was a big knocker on it shaped like a ship. Norman knocked. The noise went echoing through the sky just like thunder, and frightened the two children.

'Come in!' called a deep voice from inside the castle. Norman pushed open the door and went in. He found himself in a great high room full of a pale silvery light that looked like moonlight. Sitting at a table, frowning hard, was a giant.

He was very, very big, so big that Jill wondered if he could possibly stand upright in the high room. He was sucking a pencil and looking crossly at a book in front of him.

'Good morning,' said Norman politely.

'It isn't a good morning at all,' said the giant snappily. 'It's a bad morning. One of the very worst. I can't get these sums right again.'

'Well, bad morning, then,' said Jill. 'We've come to ask your help.'

'I'm not helping anyone today,' growled the giant. 'I tell you I can't get these sums right. Go away.'

'We *must* get his help,' whispered Norman to Jill. 'We'll keep on trying.'

'What sums are they?' Jill asked the giant. To her great surprise High-Hat suddenly picked her up in his great hand and set her by him on the table. When she had got over her fright Jill looked at the giant's book.

She nearly laughed out loud when she saw the sums that were puzzling the giant. This was one of them: 'If two hens, four dogs and one giant went for a walk together, how many legs would you see?'

'I'll tell you the answer to that,' she said. 'It's twenty-two!'

The giant turned to the end of the book and looked. 'Yes!' he said in astonishment. 'You're right! But how did you know that? Do another sum, please.'

Jill did all the sums. They were very easy indeed. The giant wrote down the answers in enormous figures, and then sucked his pencil whilst Jill thought of the next one.

When they were all finished Norman thought it was time to ask for help again.

'Could you help us now?' he asked. 'We've helped you, you know.'

'I tell you, this is one of my bad mornings,' said the giant crossly. 'I never help people on a bad morning. Please go away, and shut the door after you.'

Jill and Norman stared at him in despair. What a nasty giant he was, after all the help they had given him too! It really was too bad.

'I don't believe you know any magic at all!' said Jill. 'You're just a fraud! Why, you couldn't even do easy sums!'

The giant frowned till the children could scarcely see his big saucer-like blue eyes. Then he jumped up in a rage and hit his head hard against the ceiling. He sat down again.

'For saying a rude thing like that I will punish you!' he growled, in a thunderous voice. 'Now listen! You can sit there all the year long and ask me to do one thing after another so that I can show you my power—and the first time you can't think of anything I'll turn you into ladybirds!'

Goodness! Jill and Norman turned quite pale. But Norman took the little brown mouse out of his pocket and showed it to the giant.

'You couldn't possibly turn this mouse into a puppy-dog, I'm sure!' he cried.

The giant gave a snort and banged his hand on the table. 'Homminy, tinkabooroyillabee, juteray bong!' he cried, and as soon as the magic words were said, hey presto, the little mouse grew bigger and bigger and bigger, and there was puppy-dog Pincher again, as large as life, and full of joy at being able to run and jump again. But the giant left the children no time to be glad.

'Next thing, please!' he cried.

'Go to the moon and back!' cried Jill suddenly. In a moment High-Hat had vanished completely.

'Quick, he's gone to the moon!' cried Jill. 'Come on, Norman, we'll escape before he comes back!'

Out of the castle door they ran, Pincher scampering after them. The two pigs were patiently waiting outside on the rainbow at the bottom of the castle steps. Jill and Norman jumped on their backs, Norman carrying the puppy in his arms, Then quickly the flying pigs rose into the air and flew back to the end of the rainbow.

Just as they got there they heard a tremendous noise far up in the air.

'It's the giant, come back from the moon!' said Jill. 'Goodness, what a noise he's making! It sounds like a thunderstorm.'

The pixie came running to meet them.

'Is that High-Hat making all that noise?' she asked, looking frightened. 'Give the pigs back to Dumpy, and climb into my house again with me. The next thing that happens will be High-Hat sliding down the rainbow after you, and we'd better be gone before he arrives. He'll be in a dreadful temper!'

The pigs were given back to the twinkling gnome, and then the children climbed into the walking house with the pixie and Pincher. Off they went at a great rate, far faster than before. Pincher couldn't understand it. He began to bark and that annoyed the grandfather clock very much.

'I'm so sorry,' said the pixie. 'It's a very bad-mannered clock. I only keep it because it's been in my family for so many years. By the way, where do you want to go to?'

'Oh, home, please!' begged the children.

'Right!' said the pixie. Just as she said that there came the sound of a most tremendous BUMP, and the whole earth shook and shivered.

'There! That's the giant slid down the rainbow!' said the pixie. 'I knew he would bump himself.'

The house went on and on. When it came to a sunshiny stretch of road it skipped as if it were happy.

'Here you are!' suddenly cried the pixie, opening her door. And sure enough, there they were! They were in their very own garden at home!

The children jumped out and turned to call Pincher, who was barking in excitement. 'Good-bye, good-bye!' called the pixie.

The little house ran off, and the children watched it go. What an adventure they had had! And thank goodness Pincher wasn't a mouse any longer, but a jolly, jumping puppy-dog!

'Come on, Pincher!' cried Norman. 'Come and tell Mother all about your great adventure!'

Off they went and, dear me, Mother was surprised to hear their strange and exciting story!

Little Walking House

The End

Other titles in this series:

More Adventures on Willow Farm

Join siblings Rory, Sheila, Benjy and Penny once
more for further adventures on Willow Farm.

As the children say, a farm has its ups and downs,
and you're invited to follow them as they
buy new animals, including the pet dog True and the
troublesome bull Stamper, fight a fire that threatens to
ruin the farm, rescue Darling the horse from
illness and work together to ensure the
family farm is a success.

The Brer Rabbit Book

There's nothing the naughty Brer Rabbit
likes more than getting into mischief, and
he finds himself in plenty of it in Enid Blyton's
The Brer Rabbit Book.

With over 40 much-loved tales, children will be
kept amused for hours by the antics of
Brer Rabbit and his friends – Brer Terrapin,
Brer Hare and Brer Turkey-Buzzard, amongst others –
as they ensure they're not caught out by the wily
Brer Wolf, Brer Fox and Brer Bear.

Brer Rabbit's a Rascal

That rascal of a rabbit, Brer Rabbit,
is up to his old tricks again in *Brer Rabbit's a Rascal*
– a further collection of over 40 stories of
– adventure and mischief.

From playing tricks and practical jokes on his friends
to plotting schemes to have his work done by
others or how to outsmart Brer Wolf, Brer Fox
and Brer Bear, these tales of Brer Rabbit have
amused children for generations.

Come to the Circus

When Fenella finds out she is to live with
her aunt and uncle who are a part of Mr Carl Crack's
circus, she's not pleased at all.

However, Fenella soon changes her mind when
she discovers the circus is a magical place filled with
clowns, magicians and performers, circus animals
including elephants, horses and tigers and
many wonderful new friends who help her
enjoy circus life after all.

Hurrah For The Circus

Mr Galliano's wonderful circus comes
to town once more in Enid Blyton's
Hurrah For The Circus.

Join Lotta and Jimmy on further circus
adventures, including the day the tigers join
the show, the time they had to rescue little dog Lucky
and the first time Lotta is able to ride her horse,
Black Beauty, while standing up!

Circus Days Again

The future of Mr Galliano's Circus looks
uncertain in Enid Blyton's *Circus Days Again*
but can Lotta and Jimmy save the day?

When Britomart the magician joins the circus as
the new ringleader in Mr Galliano's absence,
the circus folk aren't pleased. Although he introduces
new circus animals, including seals, zebras and bears,
and performers, such as the eccentric Madame
Prunella and her parrots, Lotta and Jimmy soon realise
that something is wrong and it might be up to them to
put things right.

Tales of Betsy-May

A collection of delightful tales
about one of Enid Blyton's cutest
characters – Betsy-May.

Young children will love reading
these stories on their own, or with a parent's
help, and will delight in joining Betsy-May as she
plays with friends, goes to the seaside,
explores the garden, finds a puppy, learns that sharing
is fun, gets new toys, has a party and
takes dancing lessons.

The Folk of the Faraway Tree

*'Gosh!' she said. 'I've never seen such a tree before!
Is this the Magic Faraway Tree?'*

When curious Connie comes to stay with Joe,
Beth and Frannie, she doesn't believe in magic—but
she soon changes her mind.

Join the children on a host of exciting adventures
at the top of the Faraway Tree with their friends
Silky, Moon-face, the Saucepan Man and many others.
Find out what happens when Connie is trapped in the
Land of Marvels, meet Miss Muffet and her spider,
and visit the Land of Treats!

Naughty Amelia Jane

'Amelia Jane, you are a perfect nuisance!'
said the toys angrily.

Amelia Jane is the naughtiest doll in the nursery.
She hasn't come from a shop like the other dolls,
but is home-made and has no manners at all.

Life is certainly never dull with Amelia Jane around.
The big, mischievous doll is always promising the
other toys she will be good. But no matter how hard
she tries, she just cannot behave.

The Enchanted Wood

'I feel as if there are adventures about,' said Joe.
'Come on!'

When Joe, Beth and Frannie move to the country,
they discover they are living next to the
mysterious Enchanted Wood.
And deep in the wood is the oldest and most
magical tree in the world—the Faraway Tree.

Join them on their exciting adventures
as they visit the amazing lands at the top
of the Faraway Tree.